CW01266979

Also by the author:

Sailor All at Sea
Bleak Encounter at the Cape
Parsonage and Parson
The Organist and The Magistrate

"Winsome, witty and often poignant…told with much affection."

**Review of *Parsonage and Parson* by
Rt Rev'd Dr Andrew Rumsey, author of *English Grounds***

"I was expecting something concise, well thought out, entertaining and probably rather old-school - I was not disappointed."

**Review of *The Organist and The Magistrate*
in *Magistrate* magazine**

All good wishes
Richard Trahair

WHERE IS FRANCIS?

A true-life reminiscence leads to a curious tale, blending authenticity, conjecture and intrigue.

RICHARD TRAHAIR

The Book Guild

First published in Great Britain in 2025 by
The Book Guild Ltd
Unit E2 Airfield Business Park,
Harrison Road, Market Harborough,
Leicestershire. LE16 7UL
Tel: 0116 2792299
www.bookguild.co.uk
Email: info@bookguild.co.uk
X: @bookguild

Copyright © 2025 Richard Trahair

The right of Richard Trahair to be identified as the author of this
work has been asserted by them in accordance with the
Copyright, Design and Patents Act 1988.

All rights reserved. No part of this publication may be
reproduced, transmitted, or stored in a retrieval system, in any form or by any means,
without permission in writing from the publisher, nor be otherwise circulated in
any form of binding or cover other than that in which it is published and without
a similar condition being imposed on the subsequent purchaser.

The manufacturer's authorised representative in the EU
for product safety is Authorised Rep Compliance Ltd,
71 Lower Baggot Street, Dublin D02 P593 Ireland (www.arccompliance.com)

This work is entirely fictitious and bears no resemblance to any persons living or dead.

Typeset in 11.5pt Minion Pro

Printed and bound in Great Britain by CMP UK

ISBN 978 1835742 341

British Library Cataloguing in Publication Data.
A catalogue record for this book is available from the British Library.

This novel is dedicated to all my old friends and colleagues in the textile trade of the 1970s.

CHAPTER ONE
SETTING THE SCENE

Had it not been for Mr Lucknor's kindness, the experience I am about to relate would never have occurred.

He had been my lecturer at Leeds University, way back in the days when the textile industry in Yorkshire had been at its peak of technology and output. His specialism was knitwear, as far removed from grannies with knitting needles as it is possible to imagine. His research was into the commercial production of fabric that was knitted rather than woven on looms.

John Lucknor was an enthusiastic ambassador, to the extent that his rather smart three-piece suits were tailored in tight-knit cloth to his own design. They tended to bag a little at the seat and the knees of the trousers. The industrial-scale machines which he helped to develop produced fabric about twice as fast as a powered shuttle loom.

Being so closely connected with the industry, he made full use of his contacts to help his graduate students to land their first job.

I had graduated with a BA Honours degree in Textile Management, achieving, like most of my colleagues, a grade of 2:2. Back in that era, this was an entirely respectable achievement and virtually guaranteed a job in textiles of one kind or another at a modest entry point.

Mr Lucknor arranged an interview for me with the proprietor of a respected firm of shirt manufacturers that had three or four small factories around the country that produced shirts exclusively for British Home Stores.

My new boss (the interview having been successful) was Mr Nicolas Hoffmann, the owner of L F & K Hoffmann Ltd, and I was to start working for him at his plant on a bleak industrial estate in Essex.

Mr Nicolas, as he was known and addressed by all who worked for him, ruled, not with a rod of iron, but with a fearsomeness and austere authority that generated contrasting opinion from amongst his employees. The personnel manager for the whole firm, Edward, was based in the Essex factory office. He was a former Army officer, ex-public school like me, and he despised his boss with a deep loathing. Inevitably, he and I hit it off rather well, although I never came to share his angst against our employer. He and his charming wife took me under their wing, and I spent many a cheerful evening in their pretty country cottage.

SETTING THE SCENE

The chief designer of shirtings also worked in the same place, which I suppose was the manufacturing headquarters of Hoffmann's. Mr Nicolas and his brother Mr Daniel, who ran a separate business in high teenage fashion, shared their registered offices in a large gloomy brick building in Leyton, which I understood to be the area on the outskirts of London from which his family originated on arrival two generations previously on hasty flight from antisemitic purges somewhere in Eastern Europe. (Mr Daniel was a very different character from his sibling. He was quite flashy and rather handsome, occasionally turning up at the Essex plant in a dark-blue Lamborghini to confer with the conventional Mr Nicolas, who wore a staid pale-grey suit accompanied always by one of his own BHS shirts.)

The chief designer, Francis, was a delightfully calm and soft-spoken man with keen artistic interests. He collected eighteenth-century miniatures and would occasionally bring in two or three to show me at lunchtime and expound their history and virtues. Francis was a Christian Scientist of conviction. He and I would have become good friends but for his reserve about inviting home a believer of more conventional Christian doctrine, especially Church of England. I could never quite gauge his attitude towards our employer. I think he stood aloof and detached in his manner of quiet courtesy.

At the opposite extreme to Edward, in virtually every respect, sat Albert. By the time I joined the firm, Albert was about seventy-eight years of age. He had entered the company as an apprentice to Mr Nicolas's father and uncle between the wars, when Hoffmann's was a tiny outfit in the gaunt Victorian premises in Leyton. Indeed, he was something of a father figure to Nicolas himself.

His role, which he could undertake seated, was central and vital to the profitability of the Essex factory. He was the 'lay designer'. In all the other plants, and most likely at all the other shirt manufacturers, this task was done by computer, albeit in somewhat primitive form in those pre-digital days. The lay designer was responsible for creating a scaled-down jigsaw puzzle on a roll of paper, placing each and every shirt component shape onto the scaled width and length of paper, with cardboard cutouts representing sleeves, collar, back, two fronts, and cuffs. There were two essential skills. One was to match symmetrically in linear and lateral direction each part consistent with the fabric design (especially difficult with stripes and checks), and the other was to squeeze the resultant puzzle into the shortest possible length of roll. The first requirement was of course to ensure the necessary quality standard in the finished product; the second – of far greater importance to L F & K Hoffmann Ltd – was to purchase as little cloth as possible from the weaving firms and thereby maximise the profit above the contract selling price negotiated with British Home Stores. In this, Albert was past master, from decades of experience. Hoffman's was his home, his raison d'être.

Nonetheless, he was as daunted by Mr Nicolas's icy critique as the rest of us.

SETTING THE SCENE

Albert taught me how to design a lay by hand in traditional fashion. After a few months, I had learnt the ropes, and he rashly invited me to set out a lay for real. It was a check pattern of shirting, but with a strong blue line predominant down the warp. Very tricky. I was quite satisfied with my design, but of course Albert was due to check it before it was passed to the fabric-cutting department to scale up and lay on the fabric that awaited on the cutting table.

Unfortunately, on the day in question he could not come into work as he had developed a chill. The factory could not wait. Without the lay, the entire plant would grind to a halt, with a whole day's expenditure in wages and overheads wasted. The poor beleaguered factory production manager, a rabbit of a man if confronted by a red-faced Nicolas, decided to carry on and accept my lay design.

Well. Two days later, on Albert's return to his cubbyhole, he asked me to come in and speak to him. (In his absence, I had been engaged with Francis, wrapping up parcels of shirts as Christmas presents for Nicolas's friends and relations.)

Full of confidence, I joined Albert, as requested over the shop-floor Tannoy. "Laddie, you'd better come with me. I have something to show you." He led me across the factory to the cutting table, an expanse of stainless steel about twenty feet long. Along its length lay a thick mat comprising about one hundred layers of the check fabric with the blue warp thread. Two of the cutters had worked their way along about a third of the length with their electric band saws, carving out the component shapes of the shirting by following black lines marked onto the stiff paper lay sheet on top. About seven shirts could be fitted onto the table length – a total of seven hundred shirts in that cutting batch.

The waste, from the inevitable gaps between each component, was swept off into sacks by a cutter's apprentice. Three sacks were already full.

"Laddie, when – not if – Mr Nicolas finds that there are more than four sacks of waste per lay batch, my life won't be worth living. You've just lost him a great deal of money, and I shall have to answer for it. But take heart," he said with a pat on my shoulder, "you'll remember this lesson and benefit from it in years to come when I am long dead and buried."

With that, Albert trudged off back to his den. I never heard anything more.

The chief cutter, a young man named Alex renowned for his dodgy sense of humour, then came up to me as I stood there in abject embarrassment, having heard a whispered comment from one of the cutters to his colleague wondering if this university graduate had taken the wrong degree.

Alex looked at me sternly and drew from his pocket a tobacco tin. As he slowly removed the lid, he growled, "This is what happens to people who mess up Mr Nicolas's cutting budget."

Inside the tin, protruding through a wedge of cotton wool saturated in dried blood, lay a severed human finger. I stared at it aghast. Then, to my horror, the finger twitched and wriggled before my petrified gaze.

Instantly, the entire cutting team roared with laughter as Alex proceeded to withdraw his healthy finger from the hole in the base of the tin that had been hidden by the cotton wool.

The factory production manager, Ben, seemed to me a rather shadowy figure, rarely putting in an appearance anywhere on the shop floor. He was a mousy, weak-chinned man with thinning ginger hair, perpetually stressed out and frowning. He never joined us in the 'senior staff' room for coffee or lunch, but remained behind his office door, at a desk groaning with neglected piles of paperwork. My other colleagues largely took no notice of him, and it was a while before I learnt anything of his background or personality.

One other larger-than-life character comes back to me now, fifty years on. This was the machinists' supervisor, responsible not only for the efficient operation and accurate work of about seventy women and girls beavering away at their sewing machines, but also for their pastoral care. Betty was their mother figure, a large lady in both size and spirit. The girls came to Betty with their domestic problems as well as their difficulties with buttonholes and collar points. It was she who taught me most of what I needed to know about life in a factory on the shop floor. As a trainee manager, I had to learn people management as well as the technical stuff. For many months I held court at my little kiosk in the centre of the machinists' department, sorting out throughput and material supply, introducing one or two new ideas of my own to improve efficiency, and trying not to hear the often lewd whispers between adjacent machinist girls obliged to be at close quarters with a presentable, healthy twenty-two year old boy alone in a sea of females. Their deliberate smiles and cheeky come-on frequently succeeded in disarming me from any sense of authority.

But Betty was a dear. Several times she invited me home for an evening with her quiet little husband and a huge 'high tea'. I happened to know something about playing the church organ (my two brothers and I having rebuilt one at home in a barn during our teens); Betty had acquired a small Hammond electronic instrument which took pride of place in her 'parlour' and enlisted me to teach her the rudiments of stops and pedals. It was one of those keyboard devices that was capable of filling in chords automatically, leaving the player with nothing to do except pick at the melody with one finger. But she soon got the hang of all her favourite tunes from the BBC Light Programme on the wireless, recently called Radio 2.

My own opinion of the Light Programme was altogether more jaundiced. It was broadcast throughout the shirt factory from half past eight until half past four. I came to wince daily at the aural onslaught of 'Music While You Work', from which there was no escape except briefly at three o'clock when mercifully 'Everything Stops for Tea'. I think it was 'Music While You Work' that eventually drove me from factory life altogether in the end. But I digress.

As a BHS supplier, Hoffmann's factories were rigorously subjected to the regular equivalent of Ofsted inspections in schools. Once every two months, their inspector would descend on us in all her majesty and closet herself with Mr Nicolas in the manager's office to scrutinise the paperwork and discuss any current issues. They would both then come out onto the shop floor in somewhat forced bonhomie to greet Betty and me. That was the moment of truth. The inspector's main objective was to be satisfied with the quality of the shirts bearing her company's label. The routine was invariable. After a short preamble she would get out her tape measure and Mr Nicolas would instruct me to go and fetch at random from the Despatch store a finished shirt in its sealed cellophane packet. The open door to Despatch was readily visible to the inspector, who watched as I plucked a shirt packet from within one of the piles lying on the shelves. The inspector would then lay it out on a table, unpack it, and remove the collar stiffener, cardboard liner, pins and clips, and spread the shirt out flat. She would study it closely for symmetry, matching pattern on fronts and collar, and look for any wavering seams or poor stitching. Then, with reference to her notebook, she would measure every length, width and component.

We would all hold our breath. Each of us was aware that if the shirt failed inspection then the entire batch would be rejected. We would have to get machinists to unpick the BHS labels from every product, and in due course the shirts would be sold through other retailers for a price that left Hoffmann's with a financial loss.

However, our breath-holding and appearance of anxiety on these occasions were pure play-acting. Meticulous as the inspector was, she must have been slightly naive. Unknown to her, the shirt that had been so carefully scrutinised had been cut, made-up and stitched as a bespoke item by our most capable team. Once packaged, it was inserted into the pile in Despatch with a small paper tag, to enable me, under the inspector's stern eye, to extract it 'at random'.

Had she adopted a practice of extracting a shirt herself, the game would have been up, but she never did.

That all said, I think our shirts would have passed muster well enough in any case. Nicolas's standards were impeccable.

Mine had been a conventional and rather old-fashioned upbringing. I had never been a rebellious teenager. In particular, my dress code, my sartorial preferences, had followed those of my father. Fifty or sixty years ago, it was still possible to buy collarless shirts and detached collars, stiff or semi-stiff. Under my Prince of Wales check sports jacket, tucked into my dark-grey flannel trousers with turn-ups, I liked to wear for work my butcher-stripe Gieves & Hawkes blue shirts with a flexible white detached collar and studs, set off by a tie denoting membership of the Textile Institute (a tie I still possess though no longer with authority to wear).

SETTING THE SCENE

One morning in the factory, the silvery tones of Amanda, the director's personal secretary and receptionist, sounded over the Tannoy. "Mr Trahair to Mr Nicolas's office, please." The girls nearest my kiosk looked up at me and giggled as I responded with an unavoidable expression of doom.

"What yer done now, naughty boy?" one of them called out. I smiled sheepishly at her and dropped what I was doing.

"Come in, Richard, and sit down," commanded Mr Nicolas from across the expanse of oak desk. In his abrupt but paternal way, he enquired how things were going and nodded with pleasure as I described a method I had invented for selecting the best colours of button and button thread appropriate for each of the current fabric ranges. These were the only choices delegated to the firm by BHS on an ad hoc basis.

"Now, Richard," Mr Nicolas continued, "I am not at all happy with one or two aspects of your appearance when working in my factory.[1] Jacket and trousers are

---

[1] *My own father took a similar approach to his employee' dress standards, probably the result of his being a WWII Army major in the North African desert at almost the same age as I was working for Hoffmann's. He was production director of our family firm of food manufacturers. He would issue instructions by way of a perforated memo pad, the precursor of the office email. I still have his carbon-copy notebook from 1960, which records the following entry: "- To HWJE. Re. Mr Williamson. His white coat is a size too big – it looks as if he is dressed in a marquee. Also he has a habit of not having enough buttons on his coat and of not having the lower ones done up. He must be neat and smart <u>always</u> on that job. Will you organise this please?"*

fine, but must you try and copy the sartorial style of Jeremy Thorpe? When here at work, surely you would wish to demonstrate pride in what we do by wearing one of our own shirts, hmm?"

What could I say but, "Yes, Mr Nicolas, sir, of course. I'll certainly do that."

With that, I was dismissed, but I must say I was pretty miffed. Ten years previously, Jeremy Thorpe MP had visited my prep school in North Devon, which stood in his constituency, to give the prizes on St Michael's Day. Even as a twelve-year-old I had been much impressed with the suit, the double-breasted waistcoat, the contrasting stiff white collar and the hat that had become such a trademark of our esteemed Liberal parliamentary representative. As a role model in subsequent years, he would, I regret, have been an example to avoid at all costs, but therein lies the benefit of hindsight.

A second reason for my displeasure with Nicolas Hoffman's stricture was that the patterns and styling of BHS shirts during the 1970s were almost total anathema to my sartorial instincts. They were too loud, and the collars too floppy. I would not have chosen to be seen dead in most of them. Fortunately, there was one collar pattern that just about passed the test, and one reasonably innocuous plain cream fabric with a silky cross twill. That evening, when the 'factory seconds' shop opened at quarter to five, I found two of these with the correct collar size and bought them, even though one sleeve on each was an inch longer than the other. I think one of those shirts still lies crumpled at the back of my garden workshop as a painting rag. One cannot fault their longevity.

*

When I joined the firm, I had, of course, to find somewhere to live. Essex was a long way from my home near Tavistock in Devon, and I had no time to search around before my first morning with Hoffmann's. There was no internet, search engine or Airbnb in those days.

The nearest town to the factory was Southend-on-Sea. I made an early five o'clock start from my parental home in my new green Saab 96 saloon, a gorgeously eccentric but well-made vehicle shaped a bit like an egg and with an alarmingly risky device down on the floor that disengaged the engine from the wheels when the car was not accelerating. This was an effective fuel-saver but slowing down did rely on a firm tread on the pedal that operated the none-too-effective drum brakes.

Anyhow, I made it to Southend by late afternoon and drove around looking for a guest house. Now, Southend was full of guest houses and landladies, but this was February – and a particularly bleak February at that. Icy rain, trying to make up its mind whether to transform into sleet, whipped in over the sea from the southwest. The bitter wind was whistling around the street corners, frisking last summer's discarded fish-and-chip papers into the air to wheel around and dart against the lace-curtained windows like pale moths.

WHERE IS FRANCIS?

I knocked on so many doors that evening. It was a ghost town. No landlady answered my knuckle-tapping and bell-ringing 'Come back in June' appeared to be the unspoken message from the 'CLOSED' signs on the porches. I was almost resigned to sleeping that night in the car, when at last a door was tentatively opened to my enquiry long enough for me to explain to the good lady the circumstances in which I was placed. Maybe she was impressed with the shiny Saab at the kerbside, or perhaps she just took pity on a homeless waif, but my appeal had the desired effect and she let me in.

Needless to say, I was the only lodger. Mrs Sands quickly made up a small bed in a tiny room and told me that she could provide breakfast in the dining room from half past eight until ten to nine, including weekends. This placed me in a quandary, as my working day at Hoffmann's, ten miles away, was to begin promptly at eight o'clock in the morning without fail. Mrs Sands shrugged and said that we would need to work something out.

The first morning was bereft of any breakfast at all, as I left in plenty of time to find the trading estate and the factory, leaving sufficient time to negotiate rush-hour traffic.

I needn't have been so cautious. Overnight the wind had risen to a near gale, and the rain was now horizontal and relentless. I appeared to be the only car on the road.

That evening, on my return to my new home, Mrs Sands met me in the narrow hallway in her floral apron and arms akimbo and announced that she had found a solution to the breakfast conundrum. The night before she would leave out in the dining room two slices of white bread, a small glass pot of margarine ("Butter might go off overnight, dear,") and a large jar of Hartley's strawberry jam. I was to be permitted to enter her kitchen to boil the kettle for a teabag and, if really necessary, to use the huge commercial electric toaster, a monster comprising eight slots, from which I was free to use any two for my bread slices. I never got the hang of this piece of equipment. At whatever setting, my toast burnt to a curly crisp.

"Saturdays and Sundays, dear, I will of course boil you an egg as well – after half past eight."

Mrs Sands and I settled into a steady, if less than blissful, routine. The breakfast materials came and went, and my bedsheets were changed fortnightly, but all by an invisible hand as I never actually saw or spoke to my landlady again until my day of departure, which frankly could not have come soon enough.

After five weeks (during which Southend was not spared rainfall once), I spotted in the local paper an advertisement for a house-and-dog sitter at a bungalow on a small bungaloid estate on the outskirts of a very tiny village near which I worked. The owner, a young man in his early thirties, had landed a job in London and intended to rent a room in the city, returning home to his bungalow only at weekends. He needed someone reliable to look after his dog, an enormous standard poodle, and keep the place clean and tidy while he was away, including cutting the grass on his miniature lawn, for which he kept an ancient rusty cylinder push-mower in a shed.

The rent was fairly nominal, on account of the tenant's obligations. He seemed a friendly enough fellow and so I agreed the deal.

I lived there contentedly throughout my employment at Hoffmann's and even got along reasonably well with the poodle, which was equally content so long as I fed him generously and walked him around the block twice a week.

In the event, my landlord hardly ever returned at weekends. I guess that he established a social life in London that held infinitely greater attraction than a smelly poodle and a grey concrete bungalow in industrial Essex.

As for me, how I pined for the lush green fields, hedgerows and woodland of South Devon. I was now living on a different planet.

CHAPTER TWO

A MYSTERY BEGINS

Thus far, this story has been a true, accurate and literal record of the author's first foray into the world of employment – but with one exception. For reasons which will become clear, names have been changed.

From this point on, the tale is a mixture of fact and conjecture on the author's part, indeed straying all too often into the far reaches of his imagination (or is it subconscious memory?).

It all began with an incident.

One wet March morning, Francis appeared at my side at my kiosk and told me that Mr Nicolas would like me to deliver a parcel of shirts, or what I presumed were shirts, to an address about an hour and a half's drive from the factory. By that time, I was beginning to get a little bored with my apprentice role on the shop floor, and I was only too pleased to have the opportunity to leave it behind for the rest of the day and do something useful for a change. Needless to say, there was no mention of petrol expenses for the use of my car, despite the oil crisis that had only recently hit the country with eye-watering hikes in pump prices and long queues at petrol stations.

I picked up the parcel from Despatch and was given the address of the fortunate person who was to receive the benefit of Mr Nicolas's largesse. Whoever it was must have been a favoured acquaintance, as the brown paper parcel was surprisingly heavy.

With some enthusiasm, I leapt into my Saab and consulted my *AA Book of the Road*. I was headed for Royston in North Hertfordshire.

I had some difficulty finding the house. No satnav in those days of course and even postcodes were rarely used. (They had been issued, but the General Post Office had yet to acquire the technology to make use of them. They were widely regarded as a sinister intrusion into homeowners' privacy, with conspiracy theories frequently aired in Letters to the Editor of local newspapers; much as barcodes were later to be condemned in some quarters as the work of the Devil.)

Eventually, after much reversing and several three-point turns, I spotted the house name on a wooden sign nailed to a dilapidated gate giving onto a long, winding gravel drive between abundant rhododendron bushes that led to the frontage of a gaunt Victorian villa whose paintwork had seen better days.

I left the car out on the roadside, manipulated the warped gate, and carried the parcel up to the front porch. There I hesitated. Somehow this seemed to me an unlikely destination for a personal gift of several brand-new Hoffmann shirts.

I tugged the brass bell pull, and heard the consequent jangle, muffled in the inner recesses of the house. After a disconcerting wait, the door was opened to reveal, well, nothing, until I glanced downwards and met the unblinking stare of a diminutive young boy of perhaps five or six years of age.

"Oh, hello, young man," I said. "Is your mummy or daddy at home? I have a parcel here that I have been asked to deliver."

The small child held onto the large square brass door handle and continued to gaze up at me with his huge piercing blue eyes.

"Mummy?" I queried. "Is there a grown-up indoors I can give this parcel to?"

Silence. The boy's eyes were unwaveringly fixed on mine and his expression impassive. I rather plaintively held the brown paper parcel up and shook it meaningfully.

After a further lengthy period of reflection, at last he spoke.

"*C'est quoi?*" he queried, with a slight lift of his eyebrows.

Then from the darkness of the hall behind him appeared three more pairs of wide, bright eyes set in little brown faces, all adorned with glossy black hair. Two of the children were sucking their thumbs, but the third appeared to be in charge.

I repeated my earlier explanation of my arrival on their doorstep, word for word, and the eldest child, a girl, held out her hands for the parcel without speaking.

I duly handed it over, and the heavy door was slowly closed in my face. I scratched my head in some perplexity and departed whence I came.

*

It was a couple of weeks later that I was thumbing through the local paper, the *Southend Echo*, seated by the gas fire in the bungalow living room in the company of the musty poodle, and contemplating which tin to open for my supper.

Inside the front page, a headline caught my eye. 'Vietnamese Orphans For Sale'. The article explained that police were investigating reports from unnamed sources that a ring of international criminals was abducting refugees in Hong Kong from Sham Shui Po camp, which was inundated with young victims of the ongoing Vietnam War. The crooks were charging high prices for the 'export' of orphaned children to the West, and in the process generating huge profits for their own ends. Several arrivals by boat had been discovered in Southend, and enquiries had led to evidence of child 'auctions' being conducted by roundabout means from an address in Billericay. The sale process included the circulation of photographs, and one of these had been reproduced as an illustration to the newspaper article.

Now, I was no more familiar with the facial appearance of Vietnamese children than I was with those of any other Southern Asian extraction, but the photograph jogged my memory of those little people who had stared up at me in the doorway of that creepy house a couple of weeks earlier.

I awoke later that night, at about three o'clock I guess, with a sudden sense of obligation to pursue my own enquiries into the circumstances of those children I had come across; moved, I suppose, by their innocent, vulnerable appearance and apparent solitude in answering the door to a stranger, entirely unprotected.

But what of the curious parcel? What possible connection could there be with Hoffmann's factory? The juxtaposition of those two spheres of experience was incongruous and unfathomable.

I decided that my first port of call when I arrived at work the next day was to sound out Francis. He seemed to be the man in charge of bespoke parcels.

As it happened, however, he was not in that day, having been called away to BHS headquarters in London to discuss a new range of knitted summer polo shirtings due in store in May.

At lunchtime, as the 'administration' gathered in a side room with our coffee and sandwiches, and to raise a few laughs – in his absence – at Mr Nicolas's expense, Edward invited me once again to join him and his wife

Mary for supper that evening. I much looked forward to these hospitable occasions, in which, as a naturally reluctant socialite, I could genuinely relax and be myself.

And so, after a delightful meal in the dining room of their pretty thatched cottage, we settled down in sofas before a log fire to natter over generous glasses of port and a pot of coffee.

Inevitably, I related to them my adventure with the mysterious parcel, and the possible link that I had made with the report in the *Echo*. Edward and Mary were most intrigued, and in the comfortable haze of log smoke and port wine, we began to enjoy ourselves speculating several possible scenarios that might explain the connection.

Edward, of course, promptly pointed the finger at Mr Nicolas, claiming that child smuggling was just the sort of dastardly enterprise that would appeal to his loathsome employer, and merely confirmed everything which he, Edward, had long come to expect of his nemesis.

All three of us had a bit of a laugh over this, but truthfully, of course, we knew that such a tale was complete nonsense.

I explained that my intention had been to ask Francis about the parcel. Mary asked us what sort of a character Francis was, as she had never met him. Edward, ever the retired lieutenant colonel, said he found him reserved, sincere and capable, but a bit 'artsy craftsy' for his liking. I said that I got on very well with him and believed him to be a man of high principle. As I had artistic leanings myself, I chose not to respond to Edward's 'craftsy' crack.

Both of us agreed that it was quite unimaginable that Francis could conceivably be implicated in a Vietnamese orphan racket. And yet, who had wrapped the parcel? What was in it? Why was it to be delivered by hand to that destination? If secrecy was an issue, surely the sender would have chosen to take it anonymously to a post office? What was the urgency?

I departed that night to my concrete bungalow and hungry dog, keeping carefully to the suburban speed limits in view of my dubious alcohol intake, no further forward at all in my role of detective.

The following morning at tea break, I went into Francis's little office and cleared my throat.

"Morning, Francis," I began. "You remember that parcel you said that Mr Nicolas wanted delivering to that address in Hertfordshire? Can you recall what was in it?"

"Yes, my friend, I do remember that. I had the usual memo sheet from Nicolas asking me to arrange it, and I thought that you might enjoy a day out. Why? Was there a problem?"

"Well," I replied, "not exactly, but I had a rather odd experience." I then went on to tell Francis about the incident and my concerns. He stopped what he was doing and frowned.

"Now you mention it, there was something a bit unusual. The memo simply said that a parcel was to be collected from Despatch, to be taken to a private address. Normally, I would want to check over the shirts and the wrapping of individual gifts of that kind, but clearly this one had already been wrapped. What name was on the address label, Richard?"

Only then did I register another odd aspect to this parcel.

"There was no name, just the address."

Francis turned and rummaged through his 'out' tray on the desk, which was getting a little full. After a moment, he found what he was looking for and held it up to the light.

"Here's the memo. Typed, of course, but I didn't notice this at the time. Nicolas's initials are not there. He always signs his memos or scrawls his initials. I would recognise them anywhere. This isn't much help really. It just says, 'Please arrange delivery ASAP of a parcel I have sent to Despatch for an address in Royston. This is quite urgent.' I tell you what, Richard, I'll ask Nicolas tomorrow, when I see him, if he can shed any light on this."

I returned to my kiosk, where Betty was waiting to speak to me about a plague of broken needles on some of the sewing machines.

"Long overdue for a service, those old Brother units," she complained. "You'd better go and remind the manager." Betty always referred to Ben as 'the manager'. She had little time for him and took every opportunity to make that abundantly clear.

I made my way through the lines of sewing machinists, smiling to them vaguely as I pondered the mystery of the heavy parcel. Ben looked up at me as I entered his office, his usual harassed frown lifting briefly from the sea of unfinished paperwork flooding the surface around him. I passed on Betty's concerns, to which he breathed a deep sigh and reached for a folder in his 'pending' tray.

"I will, I will," he muttered. "I'll fix it this afternoon."

I then had a thought. "Ben," I said, "do you know anything about a large parcel that was delivered to a Royston address a couple of weeks ago?"

Ben sucked the end of his Biro and his frown deepened.

"Well, yes," he responded slowly, after a prolonged pause for thought, "as it happens, I do remember that. Why?"

I then related my story but made no reference to the *Southend Echo* article.

"Hmm, that does sound a bit odd," Ben agreed rather carefully. "I recall the delivery because Amanda buzzed me from Reception that a chap from the Leyton office had brought it in, together with Mr Nicolas's note. He didn't give his name, and I just told her to hand it to Francis."

I left the manager and strolled back to the shop floor, puzzling this over. Why had the man from Leyton not gone straight to Royston and delivered the parcel himself? It was quite a long detour to come around the coast to the factory.

I had just returned to my post, when Amanda and Betty both rushed up to me in a state of some alarm.

"Richard," Betty said in hushed tones, "there's a policeman at Reception asking to see the owner of a green Saab with your registration number."

CHAPTER THREE

THE MYSTERY DEEPENS

The police constable led me out into the works car park and pointed at my car.

"Now, sir, is this your vehicle?"

"Well, yes," I replied, "it certainly is." I looked surreptitiously at the front tyres, the treads of which had seen better days.

"Can you please tell me where you were on the Tuesday before last, and your movements on that day?"

I dug out my diary, and, of course, that was the day I had driven to Royston.

"I can, Constable," I replied, looking him in the eye. "I think we had better find a quiet room in the factory, so that I can tell you about the curious experience I had that day."

And so I related my Hertfordshire delivery to the constable, who insisted that I dictated it to him as a formal statement. Once again, I chose not to mention the suspicions that had arisen from my reading of the *Southend Echo*.

After checking and signing my statement, I asked the officer why his enquiries had led to the identification of my car.

"Were the police keeping a watch on that property that day?" I asked.

"I am not in a position to discuss the matter, sir, I'm afraid." And with that, the constable took his leave.

That left me with the wincingly acute embarrassment of returning to the shop floor with a sea of feminine eyes determined to make the most out of their hapless trainee colleague, gazing at me with amusement and in mock horror at this arch-criminal in their midst.

It was, naturally, reassuring to know that the authorities were interested in the household in Royston. Presumably, they were pursuing the same line as had aroused my own suspicions. But what else were the police investigating? Had they picked up any connection with Hoffmann's? If not, they would now. More to the point, I suddenly realised, I might now be their prime suspect, having been caught making a personal delivery to the gloomy house full of Vietnamese children. The constable may have thought that my story about receiving the parcel from Despatch on Mr Nicolas's instructions was a complete fabrication on my part.

Still, no doubt the police could easily check my account by talking to Francis and Ben.

WHERE IS FRANCIS?

In this, however, they were to be disappointed, at least so far as Francis was concerned, because two days later he vanished.

*

At first, my colleagues and I did not notice Francis's absence from the factory. He was often away, either at Leyton or at the BHS headquarters discussing shirt designs. Normally, he would have mentioned to Ben or Edward that he was going elsewhere for a day or so, but not on this occasion. On the third morning that he did not arrive at his little office at the back of the works building, Edward came out to me at my kiosk and asked me if I knew Francis's plans, as he had been missed the previous afternoon at a meeting with him and Ben. I had to report that I knew nothing of Francis's whereabouts at all.

Now, Francis was a widower and lived alone with his art treasures in a spacious flat that was part of a converted Victorian townhouse in Wickford. He was not a gregarious man, and had few close friends, so he informed me once when I was admiring one of his framed eighteenth-century silhouettes of English statesmen that he had brought in to show me. Very few people in his private life would be conscious of his absence from home, for several weeks.

Another of Francis's enthusiasms was his motor car – all right, an old-fashioned phrase these days, but entirely appropriate in his case. It was an Alvis TD21 convertible dating from about 1962. I suddenly thought of it and had an idea. There could not be many of those models in East Essex. I determined to keep a keen eye out for it after work in the evenings, which were getting lighter now as spring gathered pace.

Where to start? Could Francis's absence have any connection with the Vietnamese children mystery? I decided that this was my starting point. After all, he had heard my story and had been intrigued and concerned. I had still not heard whether Mr Nicolas had been asked about the memo to Despatch. Hopefully, I assumed that the police had made an enquiry, even if Francis had forgotten to do so.

The following morning, I went into Edward's office. "Do you think someone should report to the police that Francis is missing?" I asked him. "Perhaps he is lying on the floor in his flat or something, incapacitated."

Edward shook his head. "Ben has apparently already checked that. He says he managed to get hold of the cleaning lady from one of the other flat owners. No, he's gone off somewhere. Very odd. I'll talk to Ben and perhaps if there's no news by tomorrow evening, we will phone the police station."

After work that same day, I decided to begin my own search. It was a long way, but I thought that the best bet might be that address up in Royston. Promptly at half past four, I set off in the Saab and arrived on the outskirts of the town at about six o'clock. I would have to be cautious. The police might still be keeping a watch on the house. I parked my car several streets away, and walked with my macintosh collar up and a scarf around my neck hiding my chin. I felt slightly comical, a sort of pale reflection of Inspector Clouseau. I did not possess sunglasses (few people wore them in those days), to my considerable regret.

I tried to remember my previous visit to the house. There was a side road that ran alongside the flank of the building and curved around to the back of what I presumed was its garden. I decided to avoid the frontage this time, and approach from the rear.

I found the far end of the side road by chance. It formed a crescent with two accesses off the main street. I had only gone a few yards around the curve, and – jackpot – there it was.

The Alvis stood innocently parked in a row of cars, its canvas hood closed. As I strolled past, I looked around me to see if anyone was watching and then peered in through the passenger door window. The car was empty.

So, Francis had been on the same trail, evidently as inquisitive and intrigued as I was. I recalled that I had shared with him my interest in in a possible link with the *Southend Echo* article; a reference I had omitted when reporting to the factory manager, Ben.

On high alert, I continued to walk around the crescent. Soon I came to the back wall of a large, overgrown garden, at the far end of which I could recognise the architecture of the Victorian villa. I stopped and pretended to find my handkerchief to blow my nose while casually casting a lingering look towards the rear of the house. The windows stared back at me blankly. No movement, no sign of anything happening.

I could just see over the top of the garden wall, between the large shards of broken glass that had been embedded in its stone parapet. The mortar seemed to me to be quite recent.

I wandered slowly along the pavement. I was immediately conscious that my heart was beating like crazy. Several possible scenarios, each one more fantastic than the last, crossed my mind. Was Francis inside the house? Perhaps he was hidden somewhere outside, keeping watch like me. What about the police observers – were they still around?

I needed to think. I knelt down and pretended to sort out a knotted shoelace. The obvious course was the simplest, to find a GPO phone box and dial 999 to report my suspicions. No personal mobile phones in those days, of course.

But then I thought, *well, what have the police to go on? Suspected kidnap?* Even to me, that sounded a bit outlandish. I made up my mind. Acting in all innocence, I would carry on round, walk up the driveway, knock on the door and see what happened.

In my early twenties I was far from immune from utter foolishness.

*

WHERE IS FRANCIS?

Once again, I grasped the old verdigris-greened brass bell pull and heard the bell clang somewhere inside. As I stood and waited, I stared around at the front garden and the windows of the house. These remained blind, blank and without curtains, the original front lawn a jungle of bramble, nettle and patches of couch grass. I noticed that a new close-board fence had been erected on each side of the building, effectively shutting off the side and rear gardens. Curiously, there was no garden door or gate in the fence.

This time, the front door was opened promptly by a person at similar eye level to mine, a middle-aged woman with rather wild grey hair. She wore a long nondescript black dress, and several glittering bangles on each wrist.

She looked at me enquiringly but said nothing.

"Excuse me, ma'am," I began – as one still did in the 1970s if one was properly brought up – "I delivered a parcel here two or three weeks ago. It was taken in by a young child, and as I was passing, I thought I would just check to ensure it had reached the right person. It came from Hoffmann's shirt factory."

Her eyes instantly and briefly flashed in alert, but not so fleetingly that I did not notice.

"Yes, young man, it did," she muttered. "Is that all?" And began to close the door against me.

"Not quite, ma'am," I replied quickly, and made my next mistake by shoving my foot between door and door frame.

"I am looking for a colleague of mine in the factory, who hasn't turned up for several days. I happened to see his car parked nearby as I drove here. I just wondered if he had visited you here, in view of the connection with our shirts business."

The woman stared at me with an expression that slowly changed from alarm to ugly sourness. She looked over my shoulder down the length of the drive, and in a sweep around the perimeter of the front garden.

"I think you had better come inside," she said, as sourness turned to unmistakable threat.

But I was too quick for her. The alarm bells were now ringing urgently for me too, and I grabbed the door handle, slammed the door shut in her face, and ran fast, back down the drive and out into the street.

I drew breath and walked full circle around to my parked car in the crescent. I sat in the driver's seat, with the doors locked, and debated feverishly with myself as to my next move.

After a few minutes, I made up my mind. I would drive back south and go directly to Edward and Mary's cottage and tell them everything. Then, between us, we would go to the police with our suspicions. But what was I really suspecting? Surely Francis could not be involved in any shady business? He must be a victim and not an accomplice.

At about a quarter past eight, I arrived at the cottage. Mary had just prepared supper, but one look at my anxious face and she promptly laid another place and called Edward to pour me a generous whisky. Over supper, I related in detail my evening's adventure.

CHAPTER FOUR
SEARCHES ARE UNDERWAY

"Right," said Edward, adopting his previous role as lieutenant colonel, "this is what we do."

To my considerable relief, the onus appeared to have been taken from me.

"Never mind the children for a moment. Our obvious priority is to find out where our colleague Francis is at present, and why. His car is in Royston and the fact that it is very close to the house where there is a link with the Hoffmann factory cannot be coincidence.

"We are presuming that the house and what goes on inside it, are already of interest to the police. Will they listen with scepticism to our theory that Francis has been abducted or is otherwise at risk in that connection? There's only one way to find out. What's the name of that constable who came to see you the other day?"

"Um, Smythe, I think. I didn't make a note of his number."

Edward reached for the telephone on the side table by his chair.

"999 is justified, I guess." He dialled the number.

"Hang on!" I blurted out. "I've just had an idea."

Edward replaced the handset and looked at me with a raised eyebrow.

"Francis was going to ask Mr Nicolas about that instruction he had apparently sent from Leyton to deliver that shirt package to Despatch for delivery to Royston. I wonder what Nicolas said? Do you think it is just possible that Nicolas denied all knowledge of the memo, and told Francis to find out what it was all about? Maybe Francis went to Royston because Nicolas told him to?"

Edward grimaced and muttered, "Trust Hoffmann to get someone else to do his dirty work."

At that moment, the phone rang and Mary picked it up. "Emergency services here. We received a call at 21:04 from your number with no message. This is a security recall to check whether the service is still required."

"Oh, no thank you," replied Mary, "but – um – we may need to call later."

"Very well, madam, I will wish you goodnight."

"Gosh, that's impressive!" Mary exclaimed on replacing the receiver.

"Anyway," I continued my train of thought, "perhaps we should phone Mr Nicolas first and establish exactly what he said to Francis. He probably won't be happy to be rung up at quarter past nine, but this is important."

"I don't have his home phone number," said Edward, "but I know someone who does."

After a pause, he nodded and reached again for the phone.

It was half past nine before we had the right number.

"Now, Richard, here's your chance to make an impression with our esteemed employer. You phone him and explain what has happened. I shouldn't mention the Vietnamese orphan business, though; that will muddy the waters at this stage."

I swallowed hard and took the phone set from Edward. I got through immediately.

"Good evening. Mr Nicolas? Sorry to ring you so late. Richard Trahair here. I am with Edward and Mary Hanford at their home. Something has happened that you should know about."

And I proceeded to relate my two visits to Royston, and the discovery of Francis's Alvis nearby.

When I had finished, I waited. There was a long pause at the other end of the line. Finally, "You did right to phone me, my boy," Nicolas responded quietly. "Francis did ask me about the dodgy memo, and I confirmed that it had not come from me. I instructed him to make some discreet enquiries, and to try and establish exactly what was contained in that package. I am extremely concerned that he has been unaccountably absent for so long. I certainly did not ask him to go snooping around that place in – where is it? – Royston? Most odd. Now, hand the phone to Edward please.

"Edward, you're in charge of personnel, so please phone the police and report our missing employee – keep me informed."

And with that, Nicolas hung up.

Edward made a rude face, and once again dialled 999.

*

At ten to eight that same evening, another concerned citizen had telephoned the emergency services and had asked for the fire brigade. He lived in Gonville Crescent in the small town of Royston and had noticed black smoke and sparks blossoming from the large old Victorian house on the corner, opposite his own home. His bungalow was down-wind, and he feared for his own property.

Hertfordshire Fire Brigade had arrived quickly with two Commer engines, but the conflagration was by then too severe to tackle from ladders. The door into the east wing was accessible and four firemen with breathing apparatus entered the building and managed to search most of the ground floor. They shouted up the grand stairwell but received no answering cry. There was nobody downstairs.

Indeed, the entire premises appeared deserted. Curiously, a recently abandoned meal still lay uneaten on the large old kitchen table – fish fingers, chips and peas.

WHERE IS FRANCIS?

The fire brigade smashed the downstairs windows and saturated the ground-floor rooms and ceilings with their hoses. The roof had partially collapsed onto the bedrooms but the rafters had jammed and fell no further.

Fortunately, the rain that had been forecast from the east chose that moment to sweep heavily across the town, and by eleven o'clock that night the fire was extinguished.

The chief fire officer knocked on the doors of one or two neighbouring properties to enquire about the ownership and occupancy of the burnt house but obtained little information. Nobody knew to whom the premises belonged. Children's voices had been heard occasionally, but whoever looked after them kept themselves to themselves. The occasional delivery van came and went, and one neighbour had noticed a large Ford Transit minibus parked in the driveway on several occasions. No vehicle of any description was there that evening.

At midnight, the fire officer called it a day, and after his men had liberally draped 'Warning – Keep Out' tape around the property and across the entrance gate, they departed back to base for well-earned hot, sweet tea.

By then, of course, the police were at the scene, alerted by Edward's phone call. Three uniformed officers walked warily around the perimeter of the house, conscious of its instability. Then they made a close inspection of the grounds with powerful torches in the dark. They brushed through the thickets of shrubbery, nettles and brambles, and shone their beams up into the corner of the trees.

In the centre of the densest group of macrocarpa,

almost completely hidden amongst the rhododendron bushes, they came across a dilapidated but rather elegant nineteenth-century summer house, its cedar shingle roof still mainly intact. It sat on four heavy cast-iron wheels oriented on a single circular rail and so designed to be rotated to face the sun at any time of day. In the days when parasoled Victorian ladies took the air on its little ornate veranda, no doubt this end of the garden was a manicured lawn rather than the unkempt, overgrown jungle that had now swallowed it up.

One of the officers peered around the open entrance and flicked his torchlight around the interior. A line of old desiccated flower bunches was still suspended across one corner of the ceiling, now festooned with generations of wispy cobwebs hanging like miniature fishing nets and riffling gently in the slight breeze that had by now pushed the rain away to the west.

In the other far corner stood, rather incongruously, a modern school desk, and on it a large plastic ring file. The policeman went across to take a closer look. In the drawer of the desk lay other ring folders and papers, crisp and dry and clearly of recent origin. Most of them, he discovered, contained correspondence and documents, some typed in French, others in English and what appeared to be Chinese or Japanese. (The officer was not an expert at languages.) He called his nearest colleague outside, and together they bundled up the files from the drawer. The ring binder on the desk lid fell open, and there before them lay a photocopy or facsimile of the plans of a residence, beautifully drawn by a Victorian surveyor of much artistic skill.

From the title along the base of the drawing, the plans evidently related to the house itself. The attic servant quarters were represented to one side of the sheet, while the second, first and ground floors were carefully labelled in faded red and green ink with the function of each room.

Behind the grand staircase was marked a small door, simply labelled with a downward-pointing arrow. At the very base of the drawing was a further storey – extensive cellars below ground level and what appeared to be a subterranean passageway running away from the footprint of the house towards the east, where its delineation petered out into vague dotted lines, somewhere near the boundary of the grounds against the road of Gonville Crescent.

Concluding that there was little more to be seen or done that night, the police left the scene then, and returned to their station to report their findings, taking the ring folders with them.

CHAPTER FIVE

A POSSIBLE SUSPECT

All this I learnt much later, and from a variety of sources. But what of my colleague Francis?

The police kept a watch on his Alvis in Gonville Crescent for several days, but it remained there unattended, and presumably unnoticed.

An inspector called at the factory and interviewed Ben and me about the mystery memo and package, and I repeated my explanation of the two visits I had paid to the old house in Royston.

By arrangement with the cleaner in Wickford, two constables had entered Francis's flat and poked around, but found nothing remotely helpful to explain his disappearance.

Back in the '70s, the BBC Fourth Programme, now Radio 4, would issue appeals in prime time to try to reach missing persons. "Would John Henry Smith, last heard of in Weston-Super-Mare in August 1972, please contact his mother urgently, as his father is gravely ill." Along these lines, many a broadcast was made between news programmes.

The police arranged for just such an appeal in Francis's case, with a telephone number to ring and a reason given as 'concern for his welfare'.

A missing persons notice, with a rather smudgy photograph, was published twice on an inner page of the *Southend Echo*.

Two further weeks went by.

Nothing.

*

Detective Inspector Mason adjusted his yellow hard hat and switched on the powerful helmet torch strapped around it. He gave a brusque nod to his two junior colleagues, all in blue overalls and those new orange 'hi-vis' jackets. One of the burly constables jammed his crowbar into the narrow gap between door and frame, which had warped badly and plimmed up in the heat of the fire overhead.

Two more colleagues stood behind them, ducking beneath the underside of the main staircase that led to the floors above.

There was a wrench and a grunt, and then a screech of splitting oak against iron, the clatter of the crowbar on the stone floor, and a heavy, size-fourteen police-pattern boot slammed into the cellar door, flinging it back on its squeaky rusted hinges into the black void beyond.

The fan-action of the door swinging open disturbed the cold, dank air within, which wafted out through the doorway and mingled with the black ash dust which still floated around vaguely in the rooms of the old Victorian house in Gonville Crescent.

DI Mason peered into the darkness, his torch beam revealing a steep limestone stairway descending into the depths of the basement.

There were no cobwebs, and the steps were surprisingly clean. A white electricity lighting cable looped its way down one side wall, held up by a few six-inch nails driven haphazardly into the mortar joints. Every few yards a single light bulb hung from its bayonet fitting. There was a switch by the doorway which the inspector flicked unthinkingly, before he grimaced in realisation that the house's electrical system was long destroyed.

He cleared his throat, turned to nod at his four junior officers, and cautiously began to make his way down below ground.

*

"Richard, dear, have another slice of my cherry cake. And another cup of tea?"

I was sitting in Betty's bungalow in Billericay with her quiet husband, Ernie, at much the same time, as it happens, as the police were venturing into the cellars up in Royston. It was ten past five and – as was their daily habit – my hosts were listening to Gordon Clough on 'PM at Five PM', catching up on the day's news. We only had half an ear to the wireless, because I was at the same time explaining to Betty the intricacies of pipe organ stops in contrast to the somewhat fanciful names on the tabs of her beloved Hammond instrument.

Suddenly, I stopped speaking and bent both ears to the radio announcer. Betty had also left her question unanswered and had turned her head to the set on the sideboard. Ernie was a bit deaf and had not picked up the reference.

"Early this afternoon, Essex Police made forced entry into an address in the town of Billericay, following information received concerning the harbouring of a large number of children in the premises, and concern for their welfare. On entry, so the BBC has learnt, the police have discovered links to earlier reports of the illegal trade in orphan refugees from Vietnam. Four men are being held under arrest in Billericay Police Station."

Betty leant across and switched off the wireless.

"Well I never," she murmured after a long pause. "Well, I never did. Here in town, right under our noses."

I said nothing. I did not want to alarm my good friends unnecessarily, but once again I asked myself, *where is Francis? Was he now assisting the police with their inquiries? Surely not.*

Another thought then prompted me, in my attempt to find more links in this spindly chain of events.

"Why don't you get on very well with Ben in the factory then, Betty?" I asked. I imagine that she assumed I had changed the subject. "He seems to me to be a harmless sort of character, and keeps himself to himself."

Betty continued to pour the tea in silence.

"What do you know that I don't?" I pressed her, with a smile. "Has he a dubious past?"

She plonked the tea cosy firmly back on the pot and looked straight at me.

"You'd better ask Ernie that, Richard. He's the one that knows. Except he's stone deaf, so maybe I'd best tell you. But you mustn't breathe a word to anyone at Hoffmann's or I shall be in dead trouble."

I made no reply, thinking quickly. Whatever odd things were going on, I needed to be able to share and discuss with Edward and Mary, at the very least. I knew that Edward was as fond of Betty as I was. I waited.

"Until eight years ago," she continued, "Ernie was an active member of the Liberal Party and on the committee of the local constituency. Around that time there was a vociferous ultra-right-wing faction in the constituency, trying to elbow out the local Conservative representatives and install themselves as the Tory Party committee, promoting their own man as an MP candidate.

"That man was Ben Hatcher. In those days, he was a mouthpiece for several high-profile extremists and militants on a range of subjects, including Enoch Powell on Black immigration. I believe his father had been a supporter of Sir Oswald Mosley and had been interned for a while during the war.

"But that's all he was. Just a mouthpiece, a spineless, weak and pathetic puppet, you might say, without an original idea of his own in his head. Of course, the voters saw through him easily, and after a couple of years in the limelight he disappeared from view in the political world.

"Then he turned up here at Hoffmann's, appointed factory manager. What's that word that describes the situation? Iconic, that's it. How iconic – no, ironic – how ironic that he now works for a man who is such a fine representative of a race that Hatcher so despised through his political loud-hailer back in the late '60s. Well, Ernie never forgave him for blackening the good name of folk in Essex by claiming to represent them. Disgusting, I call it. Can't stand the man. And he's pretty wet at his job in the factory too. There, Richard, now you know what I feel. Let's have another bit of cake and get the sour taste out of my mouth."

*

As I drove home that evening, I pondered Betty's words and wondered whether there was some way in which I could relate what I had heard to the mystery of the package and the Vietnamese orphans – if that is what they were.

Did Ben Hatcher still harbour, or maybe even

A POSSIBLE SUSPECT

represent, political views that could involve him personally in some kind of direct action? Immigration of foreigners? Besmirching the reputation of a prominent Jew in the business world? Much to consider. But what about Francis?

CHAPTER SIX

AN UNDERGROUND REVELATION

Francis had a brother-in-law who had emigrated to Vancouver many years previously, and otherwise no close relations at all. Members of his Church were, by now, very concerned about his disappearance, and had made themselves known to the police and to the Personnel Department at Hoffmann's, viz Edward. (This was a period when employees of most reputable firms were regarded as 'persons', and not the faceless 'Human Resources' enamoured of employers in the modern world.) His Church met on the outskirts of Southend, in a modern building surrounded by an expanse of immaculately mown lawn and a white plastic chain-link fence. The members tended to keep themselves to themselves, being something of a sect within the traditional local community dominated still by the

AN UNDERGROUND REVELATION

Protestant Anglican Church, whose rather dilapidated Victorian building and unkempt churchyard contrasted a little dismally with their own premises.

Why don't I go along to their church one day and talk to them? I thought to myself. I might pick up a clue about Francis that could chime with something I knew and they did not. Had the police told them, or indeed anyone else, that his car had been left in a road up in Royston? Could there be a Church connection in Royston? I checked their times of service and intended to judge my arrival to coincide with the end of one such meeting, when presumably there would be several people there to whom I could make my enquiries. And so, one Sunday I would make my way down to Southend.

*

The two chiefs sat over a large table in Royston Police Station and studied the black-and-white photograph prints spread out before them.

The chief fire officer was explaining the intricacies of his analysis to Chief Inspector Hughes, with two other police colleagues peering over his shoulder.

"You see that?" He pointed. "The remains of a small electrical distribution board which was presumably installed on the first floor at a time when that was separately metered, maybe as an independent flat. The compressed fibre backboard has largely gone, of course, but you can see the old fuse box there, and the main switch next to it. The switch is clearly on. Now, do you see that short length of thirty-amp cable? It has been twisted wire-to-wire from the main switch exit across to the thirteen-amp circuit by scraping away the cable insulation. It bypasses the fuse box altogether.

"And here on this next photo, you can see the remains of a Belling electric stove in the room at the rear of the first floor. The stove and all four hob rings are in the 'on' position. But if you look carefully, you can just make out that the cooker cable has been pulled out of its thirty-amp wall connection and its positive and negative wires stripped and jammed into that three-pin socket by the kettle.

"With that set-up, and the main switch then flicked on, what do you get? You get meltdown, that's what. This, gentlemen, is a clear case of arson, well thought out but taking only a few minutes to arrange."

Chief Inspector Hughes nodded. "Good evidence, Chief, excellent. So we have an arsonist. But what was he or she intending to hide by destroying it? Mason and his blokes ought to be back here shortly. Perhaps the cellars will have revealed some more clues.

"Thanks, and we'll keep those photographs if that's OK. In the meantime, the physical evidence must not be disturbed. I have a feeling that a prosecution is still some way off."

*

AN UNDERGROUND REVELATION

In the meantime, DI Mason and his four colleagues had reached the first brick-arched cellar beneath the burnt-out house in Gonville Crescent. The beams from their bright helmet lamps flickered here and there over walls and ceiling as their respective heads bobbed about, trying to take in the extraordinary sight that lay before them.

The walls were draped, indeed festooned, with flags and banners. Around the base of the walls, on low trestle tables, were displayed artefacts of all shapes and sizes, glinting black gun metal and highly polished brass; straps, belts and boots of glossy black leather; pamphlets, booklets, paper and steel notice plates; and the unmistakable shapes of weaponry of all kinds.

It was the flags that gave the game away immediately. Overwhelmingly, these were of a dark and lustrous red colour, emblazoned at the centre with the thick black insignia of the Nazi swastika.

Three huge portraits, framed in excessively gothic gilt, hung alongside each other on one wall. Centre stage was Adolf Hitler, flanked either side by Benito Mussolini and Oswald Mosley, all three shown standing in preposterous dictatorial pomp staring down in disdain from their vantage point to the portraitists far below.

Banners of other extreme right-wing factions were also draped around the cellar – the blue, red and white of the British Movement; the black and red of the National Front; and the red, white and black of the 9 November Society.

The detective inspected muttered, "Good grief," and beckoned his men on into the second basement chamber, their heads shaking in disbelief and causing their lamp lights to sway to and fro like crazy lighthouse beams.

On entering the next cellar space, the men could immediately discern, on the far side, the black hole of a tunnel entrance, which confirmed the accuracy of the nineteenth-century surveyor's plan of the subterranean passage leading out to the boundary of the demesne on the eastern edge of the grounds.

In this second chamber there were no Fascist decorations or memorabilia, but just an old army camp bed, its canvas stained and rotting at the hems, with a filthy pillow and ancient grey blanket dumped on it, evidently in haste.

Behind it, spotted by one of the constables, had been left a cream linen jacket. He picked it up and examined it under his lamp. Good quality, and clean except for some cobwebby smears of dust on sleeves and collar.

"Hang onto that, Pete," called DI Mason, "we'll take the jacket back to the station in the hope of an ID. Fold it carefully inside out and don't let it come into contact with anything in here."

He led them forward into the tunnel. The string of electric light bulbs carried on overhead. Head height soon began to drop, and after a few yards the officers needed to remove their hard hats and hold them with the lamp beams shining forward, as they all had to bow

AN UNDERGROUND REVELATION

their heads and duck down in order to avoid contact with the dripping brick arch ceiling. They stumbled on as best they could, until Mason called a halt.

"Right, lads. Now then, I've been counting my steps, say two to a yard, and we've walked this tunnel for about twenty-five yards. That's a lot further than the eastern boundary of the garden from the house.

"We must have gone under the road – Gonville Crescent – and several yards beyond that. We'll keep going but, Harry, I want you to return to the cellar steps in the house and stand guard there. We don't want any nosy parker, or worse, following us in here while we have no idea where this is leading us.

"And the rest of you, keep alert because we don't know who or what lies at the end of this damned adit." (His father had been a coal miner).

After another ten minutes or so, the team of police officers reached the end of the tunnel. This was clearly the end, as a brick wall filled the hole ahead. The brickwork was clearly of the same vintage as the tunnel structure and so appeared to be original.

The air, by this time, was getting particularly stuffy, but they could feel a slight draught on their faces, warm and stale.

Instinctively, three of the men shone their lamps up around the ceiling, searching for some sign of an opening or hatchway.

There was indeed a small, round hole dead centre of the brick arch, but this was no means of exit. It was merely the foot of a long vertical cast-iron tube running up to a point of daylight above. An air vent.

Constable Jenkins, renowned at the station for being irredeemably contrary, was pointing his lamp down around the floor. He scraped away some bits of broken brick and dust with his toe cap, and revealed an iron inspection chamber cover, decorated with the cast name of its manufacturers, 'Cartwright Foundry 1882'.

"Look here, boss," said Jenkins. "I think we have to go down, not up."

The iron cover was prised up without difficulty. Indeed, the frame channel had recently been greased. A rusty iron ladder of sixteen rungs sloped down to a concrete floor.

Mason cautiously descended. He found himself in a modern cement-rendered dry basement of considerable height. Along one wall lay a flight of stairs with handrail, leading up to a closed timber door at what he judged to be ground-floor level.

The basement room had bulkhead lights on the walls, and a light switch near where he was standing. He switched it on. In the sudden blaze of halogen, he blinked and shaded his eyes for a moment. Jenkins' outsize black boots appeared from the square hole in the ceiling as he too trod the iron ladder. He joined his boss at the foot, and they both gazed about them in amazement.

Stacked around the walls to waist height were hundreds of loaded transparent plastic bags, all containing powder, or some fibrous substance, in a variety of brown hues. One bag at the base of the pile nearest the stairway had a broken seal, and the material was spilling out onto the floor.

Constable Jenkins sniffed and frowned. He went across and dipped his finger in the little heap of powder and licked it tentatively.

"Heroin, sir," he muttered to the detective inspector. He looked around the room. "There must be hundreds of thousands of pounds worth, street value, here."

By this time, the other two constables had negotiated the ladder and had reached the cellar floor.

DI Mason stroked his chin with a hand and said nothing for several moments. Then he made up his mind.

"Right, lads, this stuff justifies a raid on the upper floor of whatever building we're in, as there is clearly a criminal offence being committed here and we have no search warrant. However, softly, softly catchee monkey, and our best plan is to return quietly to where we started, back at the burnt house.

"There are four elements to this case as far as I can see: a trade in immigrant children, until recently housed in Gonville Crescent; a missing person who seems to have come to investigate; a nest of right-wing extremists of some sort; and an almighty stash of heroin, which I guess is for raising funds to finance the main enterprise, whatever that proves to be.

"At any rate, I reckon this heroin is a side issue. We'll go back and report."

While Mason was speaking, Jenkins had spotted a

large waste bin in one corner of the room and had gone over to investigate its contents.

Mainly crumpled wrapping paper and old supermarket shopping bags. Only one item had anything interesting printed on it. A torn sheet of good-quality commercial wrap, with the remains of printed parcel tape still stuck to it.

The print was just an endless repetition of a trade name in black on a pale-blue background. It read 'L F & K Hoffmann Ltd. Shirt Manufacturers Leyton'.

CHAPTER SEVEN
SUSPICIONS FLOURISH

The following day, I received my second visit from the police, this time an altogether more grim representative in the form of Detective Inspector Mason and a sergeant in uniform. Once again, I was interviewed in a side room at the shirt factory. Once again, I was summoned on the factory Tannoy, and again I was obliged to suffer the taunts of my machinist girls with as good grace as I could muster.

After an unnecessary reminder of the previous interview by their colleague in which I had admitted calling at the Royston house with a mysterious package, they pressed me as to my knowledge of the parcel's contents.

Again, I denied any knowledge, merely my assumption that it had contained a small consignment of Hoffmann shirts.

"Mr Trahair," the DI interrupted sternly, "I must warn you that we are now fully aware of what that package almost certainly contained, and may have good grounds for arresting you on a charge of handling illicit substances. We require your full cooperation and truthful answers to our questions. I think we must ask you to accompany us back to the police station to pursue this matter."

Silence, except for a gulp on my part.

"Well, sir," I replied after this hiatus, "by all means. I will do whatever you wish, but please may I first inform my colleague, the personnel officer, where I shall be for the next few hours?"

DI Mason nodded and told his sergeant to accompany me.

Edward, naturally, was horrified, and injudiciously adopted his half-colonel habit of barking instructions.

"Look here," he said, glaring at the policeman, "this is complete nonsense. Instead of pointing the finger at this lad who was following routine delivery instructions from this firm, you should be devoting your efforts to finding our missing colleague, whose absence from his post here is causing the firm considerable inconvenience."

I was whisked away and meekly sat in the rear of the police car on the short journey to the police station.

*

As soon as I had gone, Edward strode along the corridor and gave one sharp rap on the factory manager's office door before marching in, unsummoned.

SUSPICIONS FLOURISH

"Listen, Ben," he began without preamble, "Richard has been taken away by the police, who must still be pursuing the delivery of that wretched parcel of shirts a few weeks ago, up in Royston.

"For all I know, he is about to be arrested for something or other. Now, he and I have been having several conversations about that curious business, and Francis's disappearance, and we have come up with a few theories."

Ben Hatcher, he noticed, gripped the padded arms of his swivel chair before self-consciously relaxing into his seat.

"Whatever do you mean, Edward?" he replied, signally failing to catch his colleague's eye. "That parcel came directly from Leyton HQ with Mr Nicolas's own instructions. Surely it is our esteemed employer who should be answering police enquiries, not Richard."

"Well, Ben, that's as may be. On the face of it, that seems to be the case," acknowledged Edward, slightly deflated in his own low opinion of Nicolas Hoffmann. "Nicolas has denied any knowledge of the parcel, of course. According to Francis, Richard told me, the Leyton memo was unsigned, which is unusual."

Ben shifted slightly in his seat. "Really?" he replied, running a finger around the inside of his non-Hoffmann collar. "I don't think that's significant at all. Anyway what am I supposed to do about it?"

Edward snorted and, turning on his heel, marched out of the room, crisply shutting the door behind him.

WHERE IS FRANCIS?

After a moment staring vacantly into space, Ben Hatcher pushed back his chair and took his jacket from its wall hook. Checking the pockets for his car keys, he promptly left his office, told his secretary that he was leaving for an appointment (unspecified), and headed for the car park.

*

The previous day, the four police officers having left the heroin chamber and put the heavy inspection cover back into its frame in the tunnel floor, DI Mason addressed his three colleagues.

"Right then, back we go. Pete, you've still got that jacket? OK. Now, you three go on ahead slowly. I am going to follow behind and pace very carefully, counting as I pace, so that we can try to pinpoint which building this is, to the east of Gonville Crescent. The tunnel is in a dead-straight line, so it should be straightforward. Carry on."

It was not long before they rejoined their colleague in the burnt house. He had seen no one and had been thoroughly bored. However, he perked up a bit when he heard of the later finds along the tunnel.

DI Mason left the others and, muttering calculations under his breath, went outside to what remained of the front door, and carefully repeated his subterranean pacing across the grass and weeds of the garden eastwards. Reaching the boundary wall, he made a note in his pocketbook, made a detour down the drive and round Gonville Crescent to the point he had just left, and continued his pacing across the road and pavements. Jotting another note, he did a quick addition and subtraction to see how many of his original paces he had left.

But before him, and to left and right, the other side of the crescent was totally hidden behind an impenetrable barrier of Lawson cypress.

He walked a few yards further north and peered around the end of the hedge. A large 1930s detached house stood some twenty feet back from its cypress defences. Behind that, he could make out nothing.

The end of the tunnel lay well beyond that property. He would have to approach the problem later, in a different way. (In those days, a drone was simply a male bee.)

*

And now, here the DI was again, interviewing me across a table in the police station, attended by a very attractive WPC taking notes. I gave her a smile, which she did not reciprocate.

On a side table behind Mason lay several items, and immediately I recognised the corporate Hoffmann colours on a length of parcel tape dangling over the edge.

Having laboriously repeated the story of my first visit to the Victorian house, I then reported my second visit, faithfully as recorded earlier in these pages. I emphasised that my purpose in returning was to try to track down the whereabouts of my colleague Francis, and I explained the rather scary reception I had from the woman at the door.

I could tell that this rather impressed the WPC notetaker. She began to look at me as though I might be a human being after all.

Then Mason brought forward the pile of brown wrapping paper with the Hoffmann lettering.

"Seen this before?" he enquired.

"A great many times, sir, yes. It is what we use to wrap shirtings to send or deliver to Mr Nicolas's friends and relations. Probably one of these a week, and more at Christmas."

"And what about the package you delivered to the address in Royston?"

"Exactly the same, sir."

Mason paused for thought. Then he reached behind him and picked up from the side table a bundle of fabric, showing shiny light-blue silk linings. He turned the garment inside out to reveal a cream linen jacket.

"Hey!" I burst out. "That's Francis's work jacket. I'd know it anywhere – look, it's got his red-and-gold handkerchief in the breast pocket. Where did you find that?"

*

SUSPICIONS FLOURISH

The police let me go. Thankfully, I did not appear to be a suspect any longer. In fact, the WPC offered to give me a lift back to the factory, which I gratefully accepted. I think that by then she felt rather sorry for me.

I was, of course, highly intrigued by what I had been shown during my interview. The Hoffmann parcel tape and wrapping paper must evidently have been found in the burnt house – the parcel, I had delivered. The detective inspector had declined to tell me whether they had discovered its contents.

But where had they found Francis's jacket? In the house, or somewhere quite different?

"I'm asking the questions, young man. Your job is to answer them."

Well, I thought to myself later that day, *blow that*. Now's the time to go and make some enquiries myself, with Francis's Church colleagues in Southend.

The next Sunday morning, I duly turned up, and well in time for their service. I was warmly welcomed but found the experience singularly unfamiliar. They sang hymns, but mostly the hour was spent with members of the congregation standing up to report a variety of illnesses and conditions that they believed to have been healed by prayer, and without seeking any medical treatment.

The leader was known as First Reader. He and the Second Reader read from the King James Bible, with excerpts from the writings of the Church's founder in America. At the end of the service, we all gathered at the back, and I approached the Second Reader, an affable-looking chap who seemed approachable.

"Hello," I said. "I was very interested in your service. I'm CofE myself, but I do admire your confident faith. I'm really here, though, to get some help.

"I am a work colleague of Francis Patten at Hoffmann's shirt factory. I expect you know that he has disappeared, and—"

"Let me stop you there, my friend," interrupted the Second Reader, taking my elbow. "The person you need to speak to is Robert, our Church clerk. He and Francis are good friends, and Robert can probably help you more than I can. We are all dismayed and puzzled about Francis vanishing like this."

He steered me across the woodblock floor to a small, red-haired man who was clutching a notebook, in deep conversation with a colleague who I later learnt was the Church treasurer.

"Bob, this young visitor is enquiring about Francis. He works with him at Hoffmann's," my guide broke in. "He'd like a word, if that's OK."

Robert shook my hand and led me over to a corner of the room. I explained as best I could my visits to Royston, and my interviews with the police.

"He's obviously been kidnapped," I concluded, "but by whom, and why? The police didn't let on much, but clearly they must think the same. Francis seems to have done what I tried to do – to find out what was going on at the house that subsequently burnt down in Royston.

SUSPICIONS FLOURISH

"But why would Francis want to go there himself to investigate? Did he feel some sort of responsibility for the package of shirts that he sent me to Royston to deliver? Or was he, like me, simply curious?"

Robert said nothing for several moments. He had turned away while I was speaking and gazed unseeingly out of the tall window onto the mown grass outside.

"Well now, Richard," he responded after a while, "as you have a great deal of information on all this already, in fact, far more than I had, I'm going to be frank with you and ask you to be discreet.

"My son Roy and his family also live here in Southend, and he is a journalist on the staff of the local rag, the *Southend Echo*. That is always full of community gossip as well as local news, and Roy has his finger on a good deal of goings-on below the radar.

"Some months ago, he discovered a major criminal scam involving refugee children from the Vietnam War being 'bought' from a camp in Hong Kong, where their families had fled to, and arriving here to be sold off again for illegal adoption to childless couples in Britain, desperate to have a family."

"Yes," I broke in, "I remember the article in the paper."

"Well," Robert continued, "Roy helped the police take up that case, and, in fact, only recently there have been some arrests up in Billericay.

"Now, Roy tells me a lot about his work, and as Francis and I are good friends, I sometimes chat to him about some of the local shenanigans that Roy unearths. I probably let on more than I should do.

"What you've just told me rings a bell about that story. Roy learnt from the police that they were keeping an eye on a property up in Royston in Hertfordshire. I must have mentioned that to Francis, who maybe made a link with the delivery address of that odd Hoffmann package.

"Richard, I guess that could be the answer to your question."

CHAPTER EIGHT

A DELIGHTFUL PARTNERSHIP

The next day, Monday morning, I walked into Reception at eleven o'clock tea break and hovered at the end of Amanda's desk with my mug of tea. Amanda, who had been head girl at Chesham Grammar School, had a welcoming aspect that appealed to many a visitor to the shirt factory; and to important guests of Mr Nicolas in her additional capacity as his personal private secretary when he was at the Essex premises.

For me, her appeal went much further. I had become rather attracted to her, but had yet to summon the courage to 'ask her out' (which is largely what a romance amounted to in those days, within my constrained social background).

She was poised and elegant, slim and utterly delightful.

I think she had some sympathy for me in the face of the ribbing and giggling that I suffered from the shop-floor machinist girls that surrounded me at my elevated post in the factory. I thought some of them fancied me and wanted to get themselves noticed. I have to admit that a good many were most attractive to me too, which merely added to my daily excruciating embarrassments.

At any rate, at the age of twenty-two and hundreds of miles from my beloved Devonshire home and family, I needed some female company and, all right, a bit of romance. This, I hoped to find with Amanda.

But first things first. "Um," I began self-consciously as I perched on the edge of her desk, "do you remember that large, heavy package that was delivered with Hoffmann logos a few months ago, that needed urgent delivery to an address in Royston? I remember you saying it had been dropped off here by a man from Leyton HQ but who didn't give his name."

"Good morning, Richard," she smiled up at me from her paperwork. "Have a cup of tea and tell me what's on your mind."

I did what I was told, trying not to concentrate too much on her classy features, her ears decorated with tiny dark-blue jewels and half-hidden behind her glossy hair swept back into a long, low ponytail.

I nervously sipped my mug of tea.

"Yes," she continued without preamble, "I do remember. Factory gossip tells me that there was something a bit dodgy about that delivery, but no one seems to know much."

I refrained from blurting out that I knew a great deal. "Well, I was hoping that you have a good memory. Can you recall what that Leyton chap looked like, the man who handed you the parcel?"

Amanda drummed her elegant fingers lightly on her lower lip in thought.

"I'd certainly never seen him before. He wasn't a regular. Normally anything that comes over from Leyton is brought by Charlie in the Hoffmann van.

"Of course, I didn't see the vehicle that time. The fellow was in a hurry, dashed in and dumped the thing on my desk, said where he'd come from and left me the envelope which I sent in to Francis. Then he dashed out again."

She screwed up her charming retroussé nose and looked up at me.

"He was about your height, Richard, but with very short black hair which stuck up off his head like a hedgehog. Quite sallow, I think, with heavy black eyebrows. Yes, and ears that reminded me a bit of Prince Charles; you know, sticking out."

"Quite distinctive, then," I mused. "You'd recognise him again?"

"I think so, probably... Oh, and he was wearing a dark-red cardie, I've just remembered. You know, that sort with big leather buttons and narrow matching lapels. My dad's gardener wears them."

"Maybe he didn't come from Leyton at all," I said. "Perhaps he was quite local. Mr Nicolas didn't send that parcel, you know. He denies all knowledge of it. The police have found it, by the way. I saw the packaging in the police station. I've no idea what was in it, but I bet it wasn't Hoffmann shirts."

"Richard," Amanda exclaimed excitedly. "What have you been up to, you secretive boy. Helping the police with their enquiries? Have you been arrested?"

Suddenly, I knew. This was my golden opportunity.

"Um, listen," I faltered, "if you'd like to come for a drink after work, I'll tell you the whole story – well, the bits of it that I've managed to pick up so far. That is… if you have nothing better to do this evening. I expect you're busy."

To my surprise and delight, her eyes lit up and she looked at me with unfeigned admiration.

"Goodness, Richard, I'd love to. This sounds terribly exciting."

The prospect sounded exciting to me too, but for a quite different reason.

*

Meanwhile, the Hertfordshire Police had been briefed by their Essex colleague, Detective Inspector Mason, and took over the investigation of the subterranean heroin stash in Royston.

DI Mason and his officers resumed their search for Francis Patten back in the Southend area, where they thought he was most likely to be held. I assumed that's what they did, anyway.

A DELIGHTFUL PARTNERSHIP

The four men arrested in Billericay the previous month had been interrogated closely about the earlier reports of several children living in the premises. By the time the police had entered the house, however, there were no children to be found. Once again, a local constable had knocked on some neighbouring doors to ask for eyewitness evidence, but again all that had recently been seen had been a large Ford Transit minibus on the concrete driveway, and that too had now gone. Clearly the children had been bussed away to yet another destination.

The men questioned had denied all knowledge of any children and, admittedly, the house contained no convincing evidence.

Nonetheless, following the later discovery of the Fascist paraphernalia in the underground chamber at Royston, DI Mason now recalled that two of the men interviewed had worn small enamel lapel badges with the same symbol, which he could now recognise as the blue, red and white of the British Movement banners draped around that sinister cellar.

The men had long been released without charge but had been kept under periodic surveillance. Only one had been a resident of the house concerned, but the other three lived nearby.

Was Francis Patten being held by one of them?

*

At half past six that Monday, I sat at a corner table in the saloon bar of the Chequers pub in Billericay High Street, nervously nursing my pint.

Would she turn up? Perhaps she had forgotten and gone out with her smart friends instead.

I took another sip and looked around me. It was early, of course, and the place was not very busy. The public bar across the passage was doing good business, however, the hospitable rumble of voices gradually increasing in volume. In the saloon, an elderly couple were enjoying a gin and tonic in the opposite corner, and a couple of men in suits were engrossed in quiet conversation over their whiskies by the fireplace near where I was sitting.

I glanced up at the clock once again. Twenty to seven. Oh dear. Checked my watch. The bartender shot me a glance of his own, which I interpreted as a knowing sign of sympathy. Many young men had been stood up in his pub over the years and he could spot the symptoms.

The wall clock struck the three quarter, three sonorous dongs alongside the slow tick-tock of the pendulum.

And there, suddenly, she was, standing in the doorway searching through the cosy gloom of the room to find me.

Ten minutes later, and I was well into my narrative of the events surrounding Francis's disappearance. I told Amanda everything I knew. She sat opposite me at the little round table, with her demure little Dubonnet and lemon, completely absorbed in the story and gazing across at me in what I fervently hoped was admiration.

"So, you see," I concluded, "now we have to find Francis. I'm sure the police are doing all they can, but perhaps you and I can do a bit of sleuthing ourselves. What do you think?"

"Where do we start, Richard?" she said, her eyes sparkling with enthusiasm. She reached out across the table and gripped my hand. "No time like the present."

We both lent our elbows on the table and gave each other a conspiratorial smile.

Out of the corner of my eye, I saw the two men in suits push back their chairs and shrug on their overcoats, still deep in intense discussion. They were still talking as they brushed past our table on the way to the door.

They both wore rather unusual little round badges in their lapels; bright blue, red and white.

As they neared the door, Amanda suddenly reached across and grabbed my arm. "Richard," she hissed in a frantic whisper, "that man on the right, with the bristly haircut. I'm sure he's the chap who dropped off that package on my desk space, the one to go up to Royston. See his back view?" She began to chuckle excitedly. "Sticky-out ears and a bit foreign-looking."

I stood up. "Right," I whispered, "here's where we start then. We'll follow them, shall we?"

We both nonchalantly strolled out into the pub car park and watched. The two men got into an old two-tone Hillman Minx and drove slowly out to the high street. Amanda and I leapt into the Saab and followed at a discreet distance.

Neither of us noticed the other car that left the Chequers car park behind us and happened to take the same route as the Hillman and the Saab. There was nothing very distinctive about it – a Mark 1 Ford Escort in faded Modena Green, clearly having seen better days. How could we possibly have associated it with our little adventure, or known that it sported a souped-up two-litre engine?

We all proceeded sedately up the high street and then turned off towards Penlimmon Way and a modern suburb. A baker's van overtook the Saab, which gave us excellent cover behind the Hillman, and before long we reached a turning to Glayson Close. We saw the Hillman turn in but parked ourselves around the corner.

There was a pale-green car behind us, which also stopped and parked back in Penlimmon Way. Its occupants did not emerge.

"Let's see which house those chaps go into," I said to my confederate.

"I'll hop out and wander round the corner," she offered. "No one will notice a girl."

'In which case, they would be as blind as a bat if they didn't notice a girl like you' is what I refrained from saying in reply.

CHAPTER NINE

ANXIETY AT EVERY CORNER

Ben Hatcher was a worried man. He had been so distracted by his conversation in his office with Edward that his mind was not on the job. He had missed deadlines for several stock orders required to keep the shirt factory at optimum efficiency, and colleagues were beginning to mutter.

Betty, of course, was loud in her condemnation of the manager. The supply of buttons was now down to three days' working stock, and the slightly passé Brother sewing machines were in dire need of spares, which Ben had, once again, forgotten to order.

He did not like the idea of Edward puzzling over the source of that consignment of heroin dressed up as Hoffmann shirts. Ben had thought up that ruse and had been pleased with it. His plan was to set up a delivery routine around the Midlands and East Coast, using, as couriers, members of Hoffmann's, who would be acting in complete innocence of the true nature of the contents; and thereby achieving two further advantages: bypassing the scrutiny of the police and potentially blackening the reputation of Hoffmann and his ilk in the event that the contents were discovered before safe delivery.

What had prompted the police to interrogate young Trahair over that Royston delivery? he wondered. They must already have been watching the house – but surely only in connection with rumours of the children being kept there?

Once the children had gone and, on his instructions, the house had been burnt to the ground, surely the police would have lost interest? They were only searching for children, weren't they? All those incriminating file records would have gone up in smoke, because they were kept on the second floor in that old wooden school desk. Unless some ass had moved it somewhere else. Good God, he could not be expected to keep tabs on everything himself.

Still, political HQ under Gonville Crescent and the heroin store below the villa should be safe enough, Ben reasoned. He had been careful to emphasise the vital importance of destroying the entrance under the staircase of the house and obliterating the entry tunnel before causing the electrical fire upstairs. The woman and her staff would have had plenty of time to do that, surely. Wouldn't they?

Ben Hatcher sat on the edge of his factory office chair and bit his fingernails. He was a worried man.

ANXIETY AT EVERY CORNER

*

Amanda turned the corner into Glayson Close while I remained in the car. She was quickly out of sight. *Just check which house those two men are entering*, I urged her telepathically. *Please don't walk down any further or draw attention to yourself.*

At least two minutes passed. I could stand it no longer and opened the driver's door. As I was getting out, I glanced back along Penlimmon Way and noticed the occupants of the green Ford Escort also leaving their car. Both of them, more men in suits, began to walk along the pavement towards me.

I strolled as casually as I could to the junction with Glayson Close and stopped at the corner, pretending to re-tie my shoelace.

I glanced up and squinted down the length of the close. This was none too soon. I just caught a glimpse of Amanda's pale-blue jersey before it vanished around the edge of a red-brick bungalow wall, almost at the far end of the road, which was a cul-de-sac.

I couldn't be sure, but I thought I had also seen the shadow of another person just slightly ahead of her.

My heart stopped beating momentarily, and my spine went ice cold. I stood there, frozen with alarm and indecision. *Amanda, you nitwit, what do you think you're doing?*

I started to break into a run down the slope towards the dead end of the close, but before I could gather pace, there was a scuffle of shoe leather on the pavement behind me, and then a strong grip on my shoulder.

"Not so fast, sonny Jim," came the authoritative voice of the owner of the hand on my collarbone.

Even before I turned around, I remembered the pea-green Ford. *Heck, they've got me now, too*, was my instant thought.

I stopped running and reeled around to face my assailant.

I did a double take. "Inspector Mason?" I blurted out in astonishment.

"Yes, young man," he acknowledged. "My colleague and I seem to have found you yet again in a compromising position, don't we?"

"What?" I spluttered. "No, no, it's not like that at all. I wasn't trying to run away from you – I was chasing after my... well, my girlfriend down there. We were following two suspicious characters we saw back in the pub. One of them she had seen before, pretending to be a delivery driver. We're looking for Francis, you see, and thought he might be kidnapped with some Vietnamese children, you see, and…"

I might have continued in this breathless and jumbled vein for several minutes, had Detective Inspector Mason not turned to his colleague with an amused expression on his face, and murmured, "Taking all this down in your notebook, I hope, constable?"

He turned back to me, then, with a complete change of tone. "Now, listen, Mr Richard. I know perfectly well what you are up to and have been up to for several weeks now. I might commend you for it, if it were not for the fact that meddling in this affair is dangerous and must be left to the police. What you have just gabbled at me clearly shows that you have put two and two together and correctly made three-and-a-half, but with what result? You have now put your girlfriend at risk.

"Return to your car – now – and stay in it with the doors locked until we come back from that house down there, hopefully with your girlfriend. Then I shall want a word with the both of you."

I did what I was told.

*

Ben Hatcher had left the factory shortly after I had that evening, but had not returned home, nor was he planning to spend a quiet hour in a pub over a pint of beer.

He had headed north to Royston. He could not relax until he had checked out the subterranean meeting place under Gonville Crescent and satisfied himself that all was still in order there. He would also drive round to the next street, Ashworthy Road, to the villa and talk to his colleague there. He would inspect the cellar and its stacks of heroin. Only then could he afford to relax.

He had not been up to Royston for some months, having kept well clear following his orders for the Victorian house to be destroyed. He had had no wish to be spotted by any police monitoring the address.

WHERE IS FRANCIS?

Ben found a kerbside parking space with difficulty, along the right-hand arc of the crescent adjoining the eastern boundary of the house's garden. The back of the dilapidated summer house was just visible through the trees and undergrowth.

Leaving his car, he had a shock as he realised that he had parked right behind a convertible Alvis, instantly recognisable from the factory car park, despite the fact that it was now covered in dust and specks of burnt smoke debris and had a flat tyre on the near side.

That it had been parked there for a very long time would be obvious to neighbours and road users. Had anyone reported this to the police?

Ben Hatcher felt another of his sharp headaches coming on again.

CHAPTER TEN

CAUGHT IN A TRAP

Edward and Mary, bless them, had not put their feet up at home that evening, either. Edward had called Betty into his office earlier that day, on the pretext of a query about three new girls who had joined the machinists a week previously.

On closing his office door behind her, Edward began to quiz Betty about her knowledge of Ben Hatcher beyond his role in the shirt factory. He had become increasingly aware that Ben's nerves were at stretching point over any mention of that parcel delivery to Royston; and his curious evasiveness and apparent lack of concern about Francis's disappearance was becoming too obvious.

Hatcher was a local man, and Betty and her husband Ernie also had long local roots. Might she be able to cast some light onto his background?

Betty was not slow to respond. As I discovered later, she gave Edward the same critical report of Ben's nefarious political history as she and Ernie had given me over high tea all those weeks earlier.

Edward was now thoroughly intrigued. When he arrived home after work, he tried to telephone me at my bungalow, but of course there was no reply.

"Mary, would you like a trip out in the car this evening?" he enquired of his wife. "I'd like to nip up to this place in Royston and take a snoop round myself. That man Hatcher is up to something, and I'm pretty sure it's connected with what Richard discovered up there – and possibly with Francis's disappearance too. On the way, I'll tell you everything I heard from Betty in the factory this afternoon about Hatcher's dodgy background. We'll find a pub somewhere on the way back afterwards for a late supper."

Mary agreed, and the glint of excitement in her eyes reassured Edward that she was eager to join in.

They set off at speed and headed north.

*

Ben Hatcher walked stealthily along the edge of the gravel driveway to the burnt house, keeping in the shadow of the rhododendron and overgrown macrocarpa trees along its western fringe. He could see that all the ground-floor window openings were stoutly boarded up, and 'Police – Do Not Cross' tape in blue and white were festooned all around the building.

The front door, likewise, was heavily secured, and a steel bar bolted across it.

He pinned his hopes on the nether regions of the place around the back, where he remembered a couple of possible points of entry that the police and fire brigade might have missed. The back door was firmly fastened. He scrambled over a heap of detritus and scorched timber window frames piled up nearby and now growing a fine crop of nettles.

Somewhere under this lot, he recalled, was a pair of old wooden hatch lids on cast-iron hinges – the long-abandoned coal hole above the cellar that still housed a huge, riveted iron boiler furnace that had once raised, at vast expense, a few degrees of tepid warmth into the ancient iron radiators in the principal rooms of the ground floor, back in Edwardian times.

His hands and cuffs smeared with wet soot, he found at last the handles of the hatch covers and cleared as best he could the weight of rubbish lying on top.

He gave a mighty heave to one of them, and with a groan and a screech the lid was prised upwards. He jammed it open with a length of timber, sufficient to enable him to squeeze head and shoulders over the gaping black hole beneath, and switched on his torch.

A heap of coal still lay immediately below, rising to a peak about eight feet underneath the opening.

He withdrew with difficulty, banging his head severely on the upturned hatch lid. Sweating and swearing in equal measure, he shuffled around on the ground until he was able to lower himself feet first over the abyss. Carefully, he took his weight on his elbows over the coal hole frame and then let himself go.

WHERE IS FRANCIS?

He landed badly, turning his ankle painfully on the collapsing heap of old coal. Switching on his torch again while rubbing his leg with his other hand, he examined the space around him in the beam of light.

Excellent. The cellar opened into the subterranean corridor that led to all the other cellars.

Then he paused. How was he going to get out again? No possibility whatever to haul himself out the way he had come in. Damn. He had planned to drive around into Ashworthy Road to the villa.

Only one way to get there now. He must keep going, through the cellar that served as the organisation's headquarters and on along the passage under Gonville Crescent until he reached the heroin store, and then up through the door into the ground floor of the villa in Ashworthy Road.

That would surprise his colleague who lived there, assuming he was home. A bit trigger-happy, that bloke – he would need to call out first.

He found his way to the headquarter's meeting room without difficulty. It all looked undisturbed. He could never enter this holy-of-holies without a glow of pride, and this occasion was no exception. The gorgeous red-and-black flags and banners, and the stern, masterful expressions on the faces of his heroes staring down out of their picture frames, filled him again with the arrogance and self-esteem that somehow evaded him in daily life – and which, if he was honest, he knew all too well had evaded him throughout his dreary and inadequate adulthood.

He threw back his shoulders and marched purposefully through into the next chamber and along the passage. Reaching the iron manhole cover, he prised it up and entered the room below. Treading briskly down the rusty ladder, he flicked the electric lights on with the pleasure of long-accustomed practice and took in the scene.

The room was completely empty.

Where there should have been neat stacks of pristine heroin bags all around the walls, and more stacks in the centre, there was… nothing.

A horrid fear gripped Ben Hatcher. He rushed across the floor to the flight of concrete stairs opposite, and up to the heavy timber door at the top.

He tried to open the door and rattled the handle in ineffectual frustration. It was locked.

He fumbled in his pocket for a set of keys he had remembered to bring with him. The big Chubb key was the one he needed. He had used it often enough before.

He inserted it into the lock and turned it clockwise. It gave a reassuring click.

Try the latch now. Oh, come on, try it again. Put your shoulder to the door.

His fear turned now to panic. The door was quite evidently secured shut with something pretty substantial on the other side.

Ben Hatcher yelled. "Hey, Tony, are you up there? It's me, Ben. Come and let me in."

No answer.

"Tony!" Not a sound. Only his own heavy breathing.

"Hoy, for God's sake, come and open the door," he shouted again.

Nothing.

Then the lights suddenly flickered and went out.

*

Edward and Mary reached Royston at about the time that Ben Hatcher had landed heavily on the heap of coal in the boiler room.

It was long after the end of the working day, and residents had come home. Finding a parking space was proving difficult. My description of the Victorian mansion and its creepy entrance drive had been clear enough for Edward to recognise the place without much difficulty. He stopped the car at the dilapidated gateway but thought it unwise to proceed up the drive. There was no kerbside space anywhere along the frontage.

He drove slowly down the western arc of Gonville Crescent, looking for a slot. All full. Around the back, and into the eastern section, he crawled in second gear.

"There!" said Mary, pointing at a length of pavement on the right-hand side. "Look, just in front of that old convertible. I think we could squeeze in there."

Edward manoeuvred carefully into the space and turned off the engine.

"Right, let's take a look around," he said. "This must be the garden wall of the house. Yes, there it is, in a very sorry state. That fire has all but destroyed it."

They got out of the car and shut the doors. Edward locked up and they walked on along the pavement past the mucky old soft-top car. Edward stopped suddenly, and Mary couldn't help bumping into him from behind.

"Good God!" he exclaimed. "This… this is Francis's Alvis! Look at it, plastered in dust. And a puncture too, by the look of it."

He paused. "Well, this confirms Richard's theory. Francis came up here to snoop around, just like we are now. His car has been standing here for weeks. Do the police know about it? Crikey!"

He peered in through the car window but could see nothing of interest. He straightened up and walked on.

Edward stopped abruptly once again. This time Mary avoided a collision. He turned around and looked intently into her eyes.

"Mary," he whispered, wide-eyed, "this car, behind the Alvis. This is Ben Hatcher's. I'd know it anywhere." He stopped and listened. "It hasn't been here very long either; I can hear the tick of the engine block as it cools down. Hatcher is here somewhere. Presumably over in the burnt house. What the hell is he up to? Well this explains a lot. Hatcher must be involved in all the shady goings-on that we were beginning to suspect. That wretched delivery of a parcel here at this property that got Richard into hot water with the police. I knew Ben was hiding something and was very evasive when I asked him about it."

Mary looked at her husband quizzically.

"But just hang on a minute," she objected. "I know you

can't stand the man, but perhaps you're a bit prejudiced. Why couldn't Ben Hatcher have come up here this evening for exactly the same purpose that we are here – and for the same reason that Richard came back up here to investigate? Maybe he is just curious to know what is going on, just like us?"

"Hmm. Well let's take a mosey round the grounds. Perhaps we'll bump into him," was Edward's doubtful reply.

They completed the circuit back to the driveway entrance and walked up to the ruins.

The evening was beginning to close in, and the long shadows of the towering evergreens were now stretching across the garden. The front and the east side of the house were almost in darkness.

They trod warily. The overgrown rhododendrons seemed to hem them in on either side. They walked right around the perimeter of the house and paused in the yard by the back door.

"No way to get indoors, is there?" Mary murmured. "There can't be anybody here."

Then she spotted a pile of wooden debris and broken glass and what looked like a heavy old door lying on its side, half propped open. She peered a little closer.

"Look at this, Edward. The top of the coal store, where the sacks would have been tipped in. And someone has been here very recently – the weeds are all trodden down, do you see? Somebody's gone inside."

"And I can guess who it is," replied Edward grimly.

"I think we've seen enough. Hatcher may have an accomplice hanging around somewhere. Let's go."

They stared a moment longer, down into the black abyss of the boiler room cellar in the gathering gloom of the evening.

Suddenly, a sharp voice of authority broke the silence behind them.

"Don't move! Police! Please turn around slowly, sir, and you too, madam. We have been watching your movements around this property and will need to ask you some questions. Please follow my colleague here around to the car in the drive."

Dumbstruck, Edward and Mary obeyed, only just refraining from holding their arms up in true cinema style.

Around the corner of the house they could now see a blue-and-white Ford Anglia, with a flashing blue light on its roof casting weird reflections in among the glossy rhododendron leaves.

CHAPTER ELEVEN
TOO NEAR FOR COMFORT

Now it was Edward's turn to be interrogated, this time by the Hertfordshire Police rather than the Essex force that had hauled me in for questioning all those weeks before.

Edward, however, had a distinct advantage over me. As a retired colonel with a natural air of authority, he soon gained the grudging respect of the police sergeant and the constable, especially in those far-off days when a military bearing and a public-school accent were enough to impress most uniformed services.

With Mary's openly honest countenance and contribution, it was only a few minutes before the sergeant acknowledged the frank report that they were able to give him about their little evening adventure and the discoveries that they had made.

The constable was sent off to watch the open coal hole and after advising Mary and Edward to return home, the sergeant drove off in the Anglia to arrange reinforcements and a ladder for a search of the boiler house and cellars and a male fitting the description of Ben Hatcher.

*

Meanwhile, what had been going on down in Glayson Close, Billericay, during the course of the evening? There I had been, sitting on my own in the Saab as instructed, agonising over the peril that Amanda might be in somewhere at the bottom of the road.

It was certainly a relief to know that the police were on hand. Surely they would get to the house at the far end before anything happened?

I was a bag of nerves.

I sat there, chewing my lip, for what seemed like an hour, but was no more than ten minutes at most.

At last, around the corner appeared the plain-clothes police constable, accompanied by a very white-faced girl. My heart made a leap, I don't deny it. I threw open the car door and dashed along the pavement to meet them.

The policeman was very tactful. He turned to gaze back the other way while I threw an arm around the shoulders of my friend and squeezed her tight.

"Gosh, Mandy, you've had me worried out of my wits. Are you OK?"

"Just about, Richard, yes, no harm done. I got a bit too close for comfort. I wanted to see exactly where those two men went, and one of them turned around and spotted me looking inquisitive. I think he recognised me from the pub."

The man had then strolled back to her and asked in a pleasant enough voice if he could help her.

"Well," she had replied naively, "you see, my friend and I are looking for somebody who's gone missing from work, and I thought I recognised your companion from when he called at our factory a while ago, who might um, well… have seen him around, or something, you know. Just a chance," she finished lamely.

Oh, the frank honesty of young womanhood.

She had glanced up then and caught the glint in the man's eye that had flickered for a fraction of a second, before reverting to a studied calmness.

"All right, young lady," he had responded, "you'd better come in and ask him."

She had known instantly that she was trapped. A quick look behind her up the road confirmed that there was no one else in sight.

The man had extended a suited arm lightly under her elbow and with his other hand courteously ushered Amanda to walk ahead of him into the property.

Closing the door behind them both, he then left her in the hallway and went into a room opposite. She could hear a rapidly whispered conversation, and then the other man came out to meet her.

Yes, she thought, *that's definitely the delivery van driver. Oh gosh.*

"Well, miss, I gather you're asking about a friend at work. What's the name of the firm?"

"That's right," she replied hesitantly, "I recognised you

as the van driver who dropped off a package in my office – I'm on Reception, you see. I work at Hoffmann's shirt factory near here. Only, I wondered if…" (and here she invented madly) "well, if you know the people who work there, whether you might have seen Mr Patten around anywhere recently. We're worried, you see."

The man with the stiff-brush haircut stroked his chin and gave Amanda what he hoped was a reassuring smile, but which sent a sliver of ice coursing down her spine in its sinister, mocking curl of the lip.

"I'm sorry, miss, but I'm afraid you are mistaken. I've never been to a shirt factory, and don't drive a van. Now, why don't you come in here and sit down, and tell me all about it in case I can help. I'm a senior clerk at Southend Council, in the new Civic Centre."

At that moment, the doorbell buzzed. The man broke off and went over to peer through the door spyhole. He saw two men in suits, neither known to him. Glancing back at the girl and the closed doors off the hallway, he cautiously opened the front door.

"Yes?" he barked abruptly.

"Police, sir. May we come in?"

With that, he instinctively shoved the door shut again but then thought better of it.

"Of course," he said on opening up once more. "What's this all about?"

The two officers stepped inside. The younger one, a fair-haired, freckled Scotsman with noticeably broad shoulders, immediately strode across and stood beside

Amanda, giving her an encouraging smile that was a good deal more convincing than the one she had just been subjected to.

"I am Inspector Mason of Essex Constabulary," the senior officer replied, showing his warrant card. "I need to ask you some questions, sir, in connection with an inquiry we are conducting and in which you may be able to help us."

He nodded briefly to the detective constable, who took his cue and said quietly, "You come with me, young lady, if you please."

He led Amanda firmly by the arm and they promptly left the house, walking fast back up the road.

"Far better out of there, miss, I think. We'll get on up to your friend who's waiting for you."

*

"And that's about it," concluded Amanda, as I held her in my arms. "The inspector's still down there. I hope he's arresting those two horrible people. I'm sure I would never have got out again if those nice policemen had not turned up just in time."

And she burst into tears.

The Scots detective looked embarrassed and scratched his head.

"You're safe now, dear," he offered. "Now, I need to take down both your names and addresses, you two, while we wait for my colleague, who I know wants a word with you before you leave here. And there won't be any arrests just yet, so it won't be long."

We stood there, looking intently back towards the road junction. The constable had moved off several yards, and was speaking quietly into his walkie-talkie, with his back turned.

After a few minutes, a nondescript saloon car appeared back along Penlimmon Way and pulled in quietly behind green Ford Escort. Its occupants remained inside.

A quarter of an hour later, Detective Inspector Mason walked round the corner and joined us by the Saab.

"Okey-doke," he said to his colleague, "so far so good. I've put the jitters on our friend down there. His chum did not join us for our little chat. He remained very quiet in another room.

"Now, we'll all go along to my car, and you two get into the back while I talk to you. Then, I want you both to return to your car, young sir, and push off somewhere else for the evening. The constable and I will stay in our car and await developments. Has backup arrived? Ah yes, I see them. We will sit tight and see what happens."

*

I will pass lightly over our brief conversation with the inspector in his car. I say 'conversation', but it was decidedly one-sided. Amanda and I received a sound dressing-down for the danger we had been putting ourselves in, and he extracted a promise from us both not to play detectives any longer. I rather think I kept my fingers crossed when I made that promise.

Feeling decidedly abashed, we drove off in the Saab in silence, back towards the Chequers pub in the high street. We had not gone far, however, when Amanda suddenly burst into laughter and leant her head against my shoulder.

"Gosh, Richard," she murmured, "you can certainly lead a girl astray. You're dangerous to know."

CHAPTER TWELVE

A NET IS CAST

It was dark now in Gonville Crescent, Royston. The sickly yellow street lamps had flicked on an hour or so previously but failed to cast their glare into the grounds of the mansion. It had started to rain again, the rhododendrons dripping unevenly onto the gravel drive. The rear garden was in deep murk, relieved only by four powerful electric lanterns grouped around the perimeter of the open coal hole behind the kitchen yard. The top of an aluminium ladder protruded from the opening.

Two police constables in long mackintoshes and helmets paced around on sentry duty.

Down underground, the sergeant and four more constables, armed with nothing but heavy torches and with batons in their belts, had now penetrated the corridors as far as the cellar displaying all the paraphernalia of the extremist organisation.

WHERE IS FRANCIS?

Sergeant O'Henry, a big, bluff officer of long experience, still with the twang of Southern Ireland inherited from his father back home in County Cork, was familiar with the scene, having been down there once before with his opposite number from the Essex Constabulary. So too were a couple of his junior officers who had then accompanied them; one middle-aged and with a belt size of forty-six inches, the other a strong young man who had played rugby league up north.

A pincer movement had been planned. Another uniformed sergeant and three constables had driven to Ashworthy Road. The villa there had been abandoned by its 'trigger-happy' occupant immediately when he had heard the police voices in the heroin store, back when Inspector Mason and his colleagues had discovered it. He had fled down to the organisation's 'safe house' in Southend, a large, gaunt Edwardian building that had been a Catholic convent, set in an expanse of garden behind a highly forbidding stone wall now decorated along its parapet with shards of broken glass embedded in cement.

The villa in Royston had, of course, being forcibly entered by the Hertfordshire Police, and duly locked up.

This evening, the four officers gained entry, and released the bolts and hasps that now secured the heavy door at the top of the steps down into the former heroin store. The sergeant cautiously led his men down into the storeroom. He hit the light switch, but nothing happened. The room remained in darkness, as it had only an hour or so earlier for its last visitor – Ben Hatcher.

"Right, lads," murmured the sarge, "torches on and shine into every corner. If he's not here, we'll carry on up that ladder over there and continue along the passageway. Be prepared for violence."

The storeroom held no crouching figure, and indeed was completely empty, the heroin bags having long since been removed by the police up into the villa and away to their secure lock-up.

"OK, Bert," the sergeant said to the toughest of his colleagues – a former Royal Marine who could still do thirty press-ups every morning. "Shin up that ladder, and push open the manhole cover overhead. I'll be right behind you."

Constable Bert reached the top of the iron ladder and heaved upwards above his head.

"Blimey, sarge," he grunted, "there's some'at mighty heavy sat on top of this yer cover. I can't bloody shift it."

"Well try a bit harder, Bert," was the unsympathetic reply.

The constable took off his helmet, stepped up on the top rung, and forced his shoulder beneath the cover. He tried to straighten his knees as a human carjack, and pushed with his not inconsiderable might, his face becoming purple in the process.

"Nope, sarge," he panted, relaxing after a few moments. "Nothin' doin'."

"Hmm, right, lads," the sergeant muttered, "we need to go and get a screw Acrow prop. Harry, get back to the station with the car and requisition one from the workshop, into one of our Commer vans, and drive back here pronto. It needs to be the longest jack we have, an eight footer.

"And, Joe, you're a bit of a sparky, aren't you, so go and have a look at the house fuse board upstairs and see if you can get these lights working. I'm pretty sure we didn't throw the main switch when we were last here."

His two colleagues retraced their steps up onto the ground floor, leaving himself and Bert Gosling to wait patiently behind.

After a while they became bored with standing around in torchlight and made their way back upstairs to wait in comfort in the living room. They were soon joined by Joe, who reported that several fuses had blown. He couldn't find any fuse wire, so was unable to help. (No trip switches in those days.)

The three policemen made themselves at home on the sofa and armchairs and drew the curtains against the dark night outside. They settled down to a good gossip.

*

Ben Hatcher, who had been standing on the manhole cover in the ceiling of the heroin storeroom, was straining his ears for sounds in the room below. He had been on the point of walking back westwards along the passage, when he had heard the policemen's voices.

Guessing that they would try to gain access up into the passageway, he had simply, and successfully, added his own weight to that of the cast-iron cover in order to prevent them doing so.

Suddenly, he became convinced that the darkness back along the passage towards Gonville Crescent was getting less impenetrable. Then he spotted, in the far distance, a wavering pinprick of light. A torch! Somebody approaching from that end as well!

He put his ear to the cast iron and listened intently. Silence. Perhaps that lot had given up and left the storeroom.

Hatcher carefully raised the manhole cover an inch or two and listened again. Nothing.

Hoping against hope, he dragged it out of the way and clambered quickly down the ladder. Holding his breath, he switched on his torch and flicked the beam around him. Nobody there.

His heart racing, he dashed up the steps and through the now-open doorway into the ground-floor hallway.

Voices! He tiptoed cautiously past the open living room doorway and straight out through the front door, raced along the path into Ashworthy Road and within minutes had reached his car in Gonville Crescent.

Gunning the engine, he did a U-turn and drove fast, heading south to a certain property in Southend: an old former convent where he knew he could find sanctuary.

CHAPTER THIRTEEN
AN OLD FRIEND REAPPEARS

"Edward, just what exactly is going on here?" Mr Nicolas was sitting behind his desk in the factory, having arrived two days later in response to Edward's urgent request to attend the Essex factory.

"First, my principal designer vanishes without trace. Then the police keep hauling young Trahair off to the police station. And now, my factory manager has completely disappeared, and from what you tell me is also a police suspect.

"What is more, the ordering of material to keep the factory going seems to have been neglected for at least a week, and half my sewing machines are breaking down, according to Betty. I've just come off the factory floor and frankly, if it wasn't for the efforts of Betty and Richard, this place would have ground to a halt.

"You're my personnel manager; where the blazes are my personnel?"

A lengthy pause. As Edward later told me, he drew several deep breaths and tried not to shout at his employer.

"Mr Nicolas, it's a long story that I only fully grasped a day or two ago, which prompted me to ask you to come this morning. May I sit down? This may take some time."

Nicolas Hoffmann stared at Edward for a protracted moment and then invited him with a brief gesture to take a seat.

Edward then reported all that he knew about the extraordinary events of recent months, right up to date and including the scary adventure that Mandy and I had experienced two evenings previously, and which I had told him and Mary about the following morning.

When Edward had finished, Mr Nicolas sat in silence and drummed his fingers on the pseudo-pine desktop.

Then in true dramatic style, he stood up and turned to gaze out of the window, hands clasped behind his back. He replied without looking round.

"So, our Hatcher is an antisemite, is he?

"Well, Edward, if the courts don't send him away to Wandsworth first, he'll be out on his ear from my employment the moment I set eyes on him. Not for being a Jew hater, but for abandoning his responsibilities here and virtually bringing production to a halt. I won't have it, d'you hear? I'm losing money hand over fist.

"And I want to see Richard as soon as that is done. A few weeks intensive training, maybe at the Barnstaple factory with Adrian, and I might like to make him factory manager here. I think he has potential."

Little did Nicolas Hoffmann know that I was already beginning to feel that factory life was not really for me. I was pining more and more for the open spaces of Devonshire and the West Country – and the total absence of 'Music While You Work' perpetually in my ear. My inclinations were already turning towards my maternal farming antecedents and a career in agricultural land agency.

But that is quite another story.

*

I was standing at my kiosk on the shop floor, surrounded, as ever, by the girls busily treading and manipulating their sewing machines while I finalised the list of model numbers and locations of the Brother units that had broken down and were long awaiting repair. Mr Nicolas would take it with him back to Leyton and personally organise the engineer to call.

There was still no sight nor sound of Ben Hatcher, and he had failed to turn up for work for four days now. Nicolas had needed to wade through the manager's files and order all the outstanding material and other supplies – quite like old times when he ran the original North London factory in his youth, under his autocratic, full-bearded father. He was rather enjoying it.

Betty resolutely made her stately way across the factory floor to where I was working.

AN OLD FRIEND REAPPEARS

"Now, Richard, I need to talk to you seriously, and in confidence," she declared in her penetrating voice, hitched down a notch or two in the mistaken belief that only I could hear her.

Immediately, six pairs of ears belonging to the machinist girls nearest my kiosk pricked up, and a few stitches were slipped in the process.

"In the past week, Richard, you've been away from your post here on the shop floor for lengthy periods every day, except, I notice, the one day when young Amanda at reception had a day off.

"Each time I needed to consult you and you weren't here, I found you in Reception sitting on the desk deep in conversation with her – and twice carrying on together like lovebirds when deliverymen were standing there waiting to get her to sign receipts.

"You look like two crooks hatching a plot. What are you up to? Is this anything to do with Mr Hatcher? Or are you just courting Mr Nicolas's secretary in working hours?"

At this, a chorus of suppressed giggles arose from the sea of gleeful femininity surrounding us, and my face went a deep crimson, deepening to plum when I overheard a stage whisper from Maureen (the prettiest of them all) to her neighbour, "I'm here for you, Rich."

I just looked meaningfully at Betty, ran a finger around my collar and gulped. "Point taken, Betty," I muttered.

WHERE IS FRANCIS?

*

You remember my mentioning earlier in this tale the elderly lay designer, Albert? Well, after a long interval, Albert comes back into the story at this point. He was a widower – had been now for twenty years or more following the death of his dear wife Elspeth from lung cancer. (They had both taken up smoking during the Blitz in London, and by 1944 had become chain-smokers out of sheer desperation. They had been bombed out of two homes during the war.)

Albert had lived alone in a small terraced house in Southend ever since Mr Nicolas had asked him to come to the Essex factory back in 1965. His neat little home was in a quiet part of town, immediately opposite a long and very high stone wall, pierced by only one opening, an arched carriage entrance with a pair of ornate wrought-iron gates now begrimed with road dust and wholly lacking any of its Edwardian lead paint.

Albert had seldom seen the gates open, and had little idea of what lay beyond them, as a brick lodge or keeper's check-point office blocked the view. The neighbours had told him that at one time the premises had been occupied by nuns of some reclusive order, and the brick office had held a gimlet-eyed doorkeeper who denied entry to virtually anyone.

That had all been many decades ago.

Suddenly, to his surprise, Albert had noticed these gates opposite his house being opened three times in the course of the last week after he had returned home from work.

The first occasion had been late afternoon. Albert's 'parlour' was at the street front, and his armchair doze had been interrupted by the graunching and grinding of the seized iron hinges of the gates opposite. Intrigued, he had seen from his window, through the net curtains, a small car enter with a single male occupant.

The second chance discovery had been in the middle of the night. Again, he had been awakened, this time in his front bedroom. A car had screeched to a halt in the road outside, a door had banged, and the iron gates rapidly forced open. Albert had reached the window just in time to see, by the light of the street lamps, a dark-blue estate car driving in.

Albert was not an expert in identifying makes of car, but he did get the feeling that this rear view of a blue car was somehow familiar. Perhaps it was the number plate.

The third occasion was full of action. *This is getting ridiculous*, thought Albert.

It had been on Monday evening. He had been in his armchair in the front room, nursing a cup of Ovaltine and reading the *Southend Echo*. An old red-and-cream Hillman Minx had drawn up at the kerb opposite his window. One man had got out and crossed the road to open the iron gates. He had distinctive wiry hair that shot straight up like a scrubbing brush, and ears which stuck out most regally. The driver remained in the car, waited for some passing traffic, and then drove across through the archway in the stone wall.

Albert particularly recalled this, as he too had once owned a Hillman Minx, back in the day.

He had barely returned to his armchair when a pea-green car, also containing two men, pulled up outside his window. It remained there with both indicators flashing, and the two rather stern- and official-looking occupants got out and walked across to the archway, peering in. Then one, he noticed, dug into his pocket and drew out what Albert later described to me as an "odd sort of radio thing with an aerial – he spoke into it, so I guess it was some kind of telephonic equipment." He had evidently never before seen a plain-clothes police officer using a walkie-talkie.

The two officials had then stood on the pavement for ten minutes, at which point two blue-and-white police cars had also parked outside Albert's front door, with their sharp blue roof lights ('lanterns' as Albert described them) flashing vividly in the gathering dusk.

Albert had returned to his chair and his (cold) mug of Ovaltine and had dozed off.

CHAPTER FOURTEEN

SO WHERE IS FRANCIS?

It must have been only a couple of days after Albert had witnessed these goings-on from his windows that Edward and I learnt of them. Albert did not come into the factory every day; he just did so when there was a new layup to design.

One morning, the three of us were having our regular 'elevenses' of tea and biscuits in the so-called senior staffroom at the works ('Everything Stops for Tea') and he thought we would be interested.

We were. Edward and I looked at each other expressively, over Albert's diminutive head.

"Ben Hatcher has a dark-blue estate car – an Austin Cambridge," I could not help blurting out.

Albert stared at me blankly. "Mr Hatcher?" he queried. "What would he be doing, going in there at three o'clock in the morning? He's been away such a time, I thought he was down at Leyton or Barnstaple. But now you mention it, that could explain why I thought the car was one I knew. Goodness me, how very odd," he concluded lamely.

Edward took the bull by the horns. He said to me in full colonel mode, "Time, I think, for a briefing of all ranks. Don't you agree, Richard?"

I nodded.

"Run and fetch Betty and Amanda, then, will you? We will leave the shirt-making to its own devices for an hour. Tell Betty to put a girl on Reception, and to get the senior machinist to report here if there are any technical problems. Oh, and tell Alex in the cutting department to do the same if necessary."

Albert looked distinctly bewildered. "Amanda and Betty, in the senior staffroom? What is this place coming to? I don't know what Mr Nicolas would say, I'm sure."

"Fortunately, he won't know," was Edward's crisp rejoinder. "He went back to Leyton yesterday afternoon."

As soon as all five of us were gathered around the staffroom table, I having bagged the chair next to Amanda, our respective stories were soon reported. Edward held the chairmanship of the meeting with a military briskness that prevented too many departures from the facts of the case.

"Conjecture is unnecessary now," he pointed out. "We know there is a right-wing conspiracy and that Hatcher must be part of it. Those little badges Amanda saw on his confederates' lapels, I have looked up in the reference library in Billericay, which confirms it.

"There is clearly a link between them and the abduction of the children from Vietnam, as we know from Richard's visits to the Royston mansion, and possibly from the radio and newspaper reports.

"We also know that the police are well on the case of both child abduction and the kidnap of our colleague Francis Patten, although we are not sure if they have yet discovered their whereabouts.

"And now, thanks to Albert's keen observations from his house, we believe that Hatcher's car arriving at the old convent in Southend points to the likelihood that the focus of the whole saga is now there in the convent. The police raid would confirm this.

"Our only direct interest and concern in this matter are the whereabouts and well-being of our factory colleague. So, the question remains. Where is Francis?"

We sat there in silence for a moment while we all digested Edward's resumé of events.

Albert was looking at the floor and shaking his head sadly. "What will Mr Nicolas have to say about all this, I don't know. Really, I don't know at all. Quite disgraceful." He shook his head vigorously and sighed deeply.

Betty put her arm around his shoulders and patted him gently. I regret to say that Amanda and I exchanged rather amused glances. Edward frowned at us.

*

WHERE IS FRANCIS?

In the 1970s, progress with police investigations and official reports of arrest were more rarely notified to the newspapers and the BBC, and in less detail, than is the case today with media communications. Tip-off by the police to the broadcasters before arrests were even made, was even less likely.

It was more than a week later, therefore, that news began to trickle out that three males and two females had been arrested at premises in Southend and charged with false imprisonment and child abuse. A dozen young children, all under the age of eleven and wholly unknown to the immigration authorities, had been found at the premises. The young persons had been taken to hospital and all found to be in good health except for digestive conditions indicative of unfamiliar diet. They appeared to be of Southeast Asian extraction. The newspapers concluded for themselves that these were Vietnamese orphans who, unlike many of their fellow orphans, had been 'imported' illicitly for financial gain.

All five adults had been remanded in custody.

Edward brought into work his copy of the morning's *Daily Telegraph* and showed me the report.

I read it through carefully. "Yes," I said, looking up at Edward with a puzzled expression, "this is all very well, but there's no mention of the police finding anyone else in the convent. If Francis had been held there, surely the paper would be making a big deal of his kidnap? And anyway, this was a week ago, and Francis hasn't turned up here or at his church, or we would have known –

my contact at the church promised to let me know the moment he heard anything."

"Exactly so," agreed Edward. "We're as much in the dark as ever, I'm afraid. What is beginning to worry me is the possibility that these frightful people have done away with him – or maybe he died of a heart attack when incarcerated by them. Maybe they then buried him somewhere or took him out to sea and chucked his body overboard.

"Sorry, Richard, this all sounds a bit melodramatic. We mustn't start imagining things. Francis will turn up yet."

"But where the heck is he?" I could only think to say, sounding like a stuck long-playing record.

"The police will be asking that very question when they interrogate the rascals they have arrested – which presumably include our unlamented absent colleague B. Hatcher, the swine."

"So who is going to run this factory then?" I wondered aloud.

"Ah... we will have to wait and see," replied Edward, tapping the side of his nose with a forefinger in a suggestively furtive manner which baffled me.

"In the meantime," he said, sighing despondently, "we shall be seeing a great deal more of our esteemed employer in the manager's office here, I regret to say."

With that, he repossessed his *Daily Telegraph* and returned to his own office upstairs.

WHERE IS FRANCIS?

*

That very morning, in a small room entered from a modest doorway on Gower Street, London W1, four sombre-suited men sat around a table. There were no windows, and the fluorescent strip light glared down on their heads as they perused their file notes – all of these being in plain buff folders marked MOST SECRET.

The man whose office this was opened the meeting. "Gentlemen, I have asked you if you would be good enough to attend here today because I believe the moment has come for us to implement Operation Iron Shackle forthwith. Thanks to you and your team, Daniel, we have enough evidence now to seize and convict."

CHAPTER FIFTEEN

THE SECRET SERVICE DELIBERATES

The senior MI5 officer continued with introductions around the table. There were representatives from Liverpool and Bristol, as well as Daniel Hoffmann from London. All had civilian covers, but only Daniel had a genuine long-term one, being a partner in the family business running the high-fashion side of a tailoring company.

His brother Nicolas knew nothing of Daniel's 'alter ego' as a secret service agent, for which he had been recruited at the time of the arrest of Harry Houghton in 1961 and then the exposure of Kim Philby in 1963.

The agents from Liverpool and Bristol summarised the evidence they had established of extreme right-wing underground conspiracy in their areas, and the series of illegal rackets they had discovered that financed these groups, ranging from drug importation and Mafia-style intimidation of retail businesses to honey-trap sexual blackmail of leading establishment figures.

Daniel brought the meeting up to date with the discoveries under the mansion in Gonville Crescent, Royston, the seizure of heroin stocks, and the arrest of those who had run the highly lucrative illegal importation of Vietnamese children – an innovative venture that was ultimately just too likely to be exposed.

"Unwittingly," Daniel said ruefully, "this was all unearthed by employees of my brother at our shirt factory in Essex. The manager himself proved to be the local ringleader. Nicolas is very puzzled by the whole affair, of course, but I have kept well clear."

The senior MI5 officer nodded and turned over one of his brown files.

"So now," he explained, "we are in a position to go for the big fish in the pond. The leaders of these groups in all three centres – and we must remember that there will be groups based in other large cities in England that we have not yet discovered – all have proven links to our suspect 'Iron Shackle', the evidence being, in our view, strong enough for prosecution and conviction of our suspect.

"We have also obtained clandestine bug recordings of his meetings with three very senior military officers – two Army and one RAF – at an address in Euston owned by his sister, at which the high-level conspiracy to stage the anticipated far-right government coup plot is clearly indicated."

THE SECRET SERVICE DELIBERATES

Daniel Hoffmann interposed, "Have you tested this new voice-recognition system we have been briefed on?"

"Yes," was the reply, "and it confirms the identity of those four individuals. Now, up until today, you have not been given the identity of Iron Shackle, but in view of the roles I am about to commission you with, I am authorised to tell you that Iron Shackle is a Minister of State in the Home Office."

*

You may well ask, dear reader, how I know of this MI5 session, and of course the answer is that I don't. It is conjecture on my part for the purpose of this narrative, but in view of the eventual court cases, which I followed avidly, some such scenario is almost inevitable.

Ultimately, nine men stood trial for making a treasonous undertaking with the aim of 'forcibly eliminating the existing state order.' Six of them, including the disgraced former Minister of State, were given lifetime prison sentences. At the time of my writing this story, most have long since departed this life.

Amongst other tactics, they had planned to kidnap Princess Anne and then demand the resignation of the Prime Minister and his entire government.

That is a saga needing its own book, and I must return to the more local consequences of the story as they affected me and my colleagues.

WHERE IS FRANCIS?

*

"One moment, if you please, Daniel," the senior MI5 officer murmured, as his colleagues prepared to leave the building in Gower Street.

"I need you to look into a further matter before we pounce. I should explain that the powers that be called this 'Operation Iron Shackle' for a particular reason. 'Iron Shackle' was the name of a Polish sail-training organisation back in the '60s – it may still be, for all I know. Inevitably, there has long been a Soviet interest in such institutions, and we have reason to believe that two young Soviet agents were aboard one of its clipper ships when it called in – officially unannounced – at Millbay Docks in Plymouth because it had a serious engine fault. I don't suppose the sailing association which ran the vessel were aware of the young men's subversive identity at all, and the engine fault was genuine.

"The Iron Shackle skipper had radioed from the Channel to the Royal Western Yacht Club in Plymouth, asking for a spare part to be obtained from a Bristol supplier, and delivered to Millbay Docks for handover when the ship arrived. This is a fairly standard arrangement for sail-training organisations using the Channel and Western Approaches, and an RWYC member is always on call by rota, to make the necessary collection and delivery.

"Anyway, this all went according to plan, but it appears that on docking in Plymouth, which the harbour master only knew about when he actually saw the ship approaching, two of the training crew absconded and disappeared into Britain. This, too, was and is all too regular an occurrence from vessels connected with the Soviet bloc. Most, of course, do so to escape the totalitarian regimes, but others do so 'by arrangement' with their state authority.

"Now, the two agents on this occasion clearly saw their chance to gain illicit entry into the UK, as encouraged by their masters as the opportunity might arise. One of them has been apprehended recently and has confessed. He had pretended to be a member of the National Front in order to help ferment any totalitarian instincts in people of influence. This, he had achieved with our suspect who is now Minister of State. He had reinforced his personal influence by setting a honey-trap and blackmail with the esteemed minister by secretly filming both of them in bed together."

The speaker paused for breath.

"So what do you want me to do, sir?" enquired Daniel Hoffmann.

"We would like you to find, and interview, the representative of the Royal Western Yacht Club who delivered that engine part to the sail training ship ten years ago.

"We urgently need to locate and arrest the second Soviet agent who absconded from the ship at that time. His colleague, who is now in custody, recollects that the Yacht Club fellow was a young man of about eighteen who was shown around the ship by the other agent, who was plying him with questions in English concerning life in Britain, and may have provided clues as to his intentions once in the country. The two agents parted company on escaping the docked ship and have apparently not seen each other since."

And so that meeting in Gower Street ended.

CHAPTER SIXTEEN
FACT OR FICTION?

Once again I have to admit that I have no direct knowledge of these Gower Street conversations, for obvious reasons; and you may well be wondering what relevance they had for me, anyway.

I have, therefore, to crave the indulgence of my readers for a second time, in mixing an autobiographical history of the author with his fictional narrative. Or is it fiction? Perhaps it is surmise on my part. Fact is odder than fiction. All this happened half a century ago, and I have often pondered over some unexplained curiosities, not least my brief engagement with the Iron Shackle Fraternity of Poland.

For I was the seventeen-year-old boy who went aboard that sail-training clipper ship in Plymouth in 1968.

Let me explain. I had left school that July and was at my childhood home on the edge of Dartmoor, about to start a 'gap year' engagement in an approved school near Glasgow as a volunteer teacher (and, as it happened, the tractor driver of its little grey Fergie rolling the football pitches).

One morning, in the absence of my parents from home for a few days, I answered the telephone to the commodore's secretary at the Royal Western Yacht Club of England in Plymouth, only eight miles from where we lived.

My father must have been on rota duty that day, as the RWYC member deputed to assist with emergencies.

Could I drive into Devonport to a marine engineering warehouse and pick up a heavy package for immediate delivery across the city to Millbay Docks, where a clipper ship was due to reach port later that day?

Yes, of course I could.

The package had been rushed down from the engineer's premises up in Bristol, after an urgent ship-to-shore request from the ship's skipper.

I was then to go straight to the docks (which I know well as my father kept his boat there) and await the ship's arrival.

I duly followed the instructions and arrived in Millbay in mid-afternoon with a cardboard box containing a substantial spare engine part. I parked in our familiar spot and walked around the quayside to the harbour master's little observation kiosk on one of the jetties. I explained what I had come for, but the staff there knew nothing of any imminent arrival of a clipper ship. This put me in a bit of a panic, so I phoned the Yacht Club from a telephone box to check whether I was in the right place. Yes, I was.

Well, I hung around there for hours. Eventually, when it was almost dark, with the dockside lights and colour signals all glittering away in the surface reflection of the black seawater, this huge steel vessel, sails all furled, stuttered ponderously into the outer dock at a snail's pace, to be met by a harbour tug and carefully moored alongside the quay.

Once again, I called at the jetty office and repeated my purpose. The officer on duty nodded me in the direction of the aluminium wheeled ramp, and I staggered aboard under the burden of my weighty cardboard box.

Well, what a welcome I received. I have had a soft spot for the warm-hearted people of Poland ever since. The skipper, mate and some of the young trainees entertained me royally for an hour down in the officer's mess cabin. I was fed Polish delicacies; served several small glasses of something mildly tasting of aniseed and with the kick of a mule; given a guided tour of the ship by one of the trainees; and eventually packed off the ship laden with Polish souvenirs, some very edible. I was waved onto the quayside by all my new friends, who were themselves not permitted to set foot on land.

My most precious memento was their blue-and-white association burgee, which years later I flew from the rigging of my own little sailing cruiser until its canvas triangle finally disintegrated in about 2012, forty-four years after this little teenage adventure.

I have recently tried to Google the fraternity, but there is nothing. All has long since been swept away into history.

*

Daniel Hoffmann (back into fiction now, dear reader – I think) carried out his MI5 commission most assiduously. To cut a long story short, he tracked me down after only a few weeks, assisted by the meticulous records of the RWYC and the Plymouth Sound harbour authorities, and by my father's memory of my regaling him with my adventure at the time.

No one could be more astonished than Mr Daniel in tracing me then, in full circle, back to my presence in his brother's factory in Essex. In fact, I had met him before, a brief interview in his Lamborghini sports car just as I was starting work at Hoffmann's.

This placed him in some difficulty. Why on earth would the proprietor of a tailoring business, well known to me through his family connections, be interested in quizzing me about a Polish trainee sailor whom I had met in unusual circumstances in 1968?

Nonetheless, he drove up to the Essex factory one day and asked me into Mr Nicolas's empty office for a chat.

He began by asking me about my work at the factory and my ambitions for a professional career in the textile trade. I told him that I had enjoyed my textiles course at university and had gained useful experience with the shirt-making side of the business but was keen to return before long to the West Country where my roots lay. Might I perhaps widen my management training at the factory in Barnstaple, and take it from there?

I was trying to let him down gently, but I had already decided to apply to the College of Estate Management in Reading for a distance-learning diploma course, with land agency as a chartered surveyor in mind.

"All my family are in the Plymouth area," I explained to him, "and more in West Cornwall too."

My reference to Plymouth gave Mr Daniel the opening he was looking for.

"That's interesting," he said. "I was only speaking to someone the other day about his time in Plymouth back a few years ago.

"He had been a customs officer at Millbay Docks," Daniel ad-libbed, "with some fascinating stories of the ships and boats he came into contact with, from all the coastal nations of Europe."

He continued brazenly to invent a few anecdotes from his fictitious customs officer, and of course it was only a matter of time before I followed suit with more truthful ones of my own.

By now, we were having a very pleasant and relaxed conversation over our coffee, which Amanda had brought in and who gave me a discreet wink as she left the room. It was not difficult for Daniel to get me to describe the Polish sailor who had shown me round the Iron Shackle Fraternity ship and who had been so intrigued with the details of ordinary life in the 'free world' beyond the totalitarian Communist borders. I could remember much of it despite the ten years since it had taken place.

"He seemed to be particularly keen to know about a place near Malvern that he had heard of, and tried to get me to explain how to get there.

"Well, the name meant nothing to me and I had never been to Malvern, so I couldn't really help him much. I remember the conversation, because it struck me as odd that this chap was asking for the route to a place, when he was never going to go there," I mused.

Daniel nodded and changed the subject. My description of the Pole – blond-yellow hair and surprisingly pale for a sailor, and tall too – at least six foot, I recalled – he must also have lodged in his MI5 mind.

Soon after that, Mr Daniel departed, his Lamborghini spitting gravel from its tyres as he roared off out of the works car park.

I never saw him again.

CHAPTER SEVENTEEN
ANALYSIS AND MEMORY PROVE FRUITFUL

One evening, around the characterless gas fire in my concrete bungalow home, the smell of wet dog from my woolly companion poodle permeating the atmosphere, Amanda and I sat together on the plastic sofa, both wrapped in my snug tartan car rug and half listening to the wireless.

The national news was followed by the local BBC reports. There was nothing of note.

"Y'know, all this business of child abduction and extremist shenanigans has gone completely off the map," I muttered. "There's been nothing for weeks now. And yet there's not a whisper of any progress in the police search for Francis. You and I have been firmly warned not to go on trying to find him ourselves, but surely the local villains have all been rounded up by now, so where's the risk in us having another go?"

Amanda rested her head in the hollow of my shoulder. "What's my brave boy scheming now? You want to put me in danger again?"

"Hang on," I protested, "you didn't have to go right down to that house at the end of Glayson Close. In fact, I specifically told you to stay back at the junction and just see where the man went."

"Specifically, perspifically, I do love the way you speak, Richard," she answered inconsequentially, putting her arm out and ruffling my hair. (I had quite a mop in those days). "I wish I'd been a fly on the wall at your fancy public school listening to you all talking. It would have been a hoot."

I smiled in recollection. "Oh, some of my friends had nice local accents – Devonshire, Somerset, Wiltshire. The chap in my year with the most cut-glass upper-crust Queen's English was an African from Sierra Leone who had to leave school early to return home and take the throne in his tribal kingdom. He was a great chap – brilliant wing three-quarter at rugger."

"Gracious, Richard, the circles you move in. What a comedown here with us in a place like Billericay, the pits."

I drew her closer and kissed her ear. "This isn't getting us very far in deciding what to do about Francis, is it?"

"Well, what do you have in mind, my own special toff?"

I gazed in concentration at the gas fire for a few moments. "The last we know of him is his car left by

ANALYSIS AND MEMORY PROVE FRUITFUL

the pavement up in Royston, and his jacket the police found, which must have been in or around the burnt-out mansion.

"If he had been taken hostage there, as I nearly was myself, then what did the villains do with him when they all abandoned the place and presumably fled down to the old convent in Southend? The police didn't find him there either.

"So, only two possibilities, I guess. Either they took him somewhere else and locked him up, or he managed to escape in Royston or in Southend – more likely Royston as the convent in Southend is fairly impenetrable in or out.

"In either case, surely he would have turned up by now? Unless he was so securely locked up that he's died of starvation."

We both fell silent and tried to gather our thoughts.

The woolly poodle clearly wanted to be included, looking up from his recumbent position on the nylon hearthrug at that moment with an expectant stare, clearly implying that deep thought needed sustenance, and surely it was supper time.

*

The same concerns were being discussed that evening between Mary and Edward around the log fire in their beautifully furnished drawing room. Their golden retriever lay, full length, on the Turkish hearthrug, snoring gently and dreaming of pheasants and open spaces.

"It's just ridiculous, you know." Edward frowned into his glass of cognac. "The police have all the clues they could possibly need, and have had the likely culprits in the nick for ages. Why can't they interrogate them properly and locate Francis?"

"Dead or alive," interjected Mary, giving voice to their worst fears.

"Quite," said Edward with a deepening frown.

Mary's face lit up. "I think it's time you and I joined forces again with Richard and renewed our own investigation. Remember that before I met you I was a food analyst with the county council – I'm good at detail."

"That's very true, and with a first-class degree to prove it, unlike your dull old husband who only scraped through Sandhurst with pure bluff. Of course, if we enlist Richard we will now also get Amanda as a bolt-on, won't we?"

"Edward, don't be so unkind. I think it's rather sweet. And they've both proved their mettle before. Either of them could have been in Francis's position, languishing in the villains' den under lock and key. Have a word with Richard tomorrow, and we'll put our heads together."

And so it was that a couple of days later, after the factory had shut and Mr Nicolas had returned to his hotel where he had booked a suite while he managed the factory, the four of us sat around the corner table in the Chequers and pooled our ideas.

ANALYSIS AND MEMORY PROVE FRUITFUL

Mary, the analyst, drew up on her notepad four columns under the headings 'Known', 'Possible', 'Likely' and 'Action'. The first two categories were soon completed, and from the 'Possibles', the forensic team began to list the 'Likelys' according to the strength of evidence.

Francis had clearly been trapped at Royston. Why had he gone there in the first place? Unlike the four of us, he did not strike one as a particularly adventurous character. He was on mutually respected terms with Nicolas Hoffmann, and would surely have consulted his boss before trying to follow up my story of the dodgy delivery to the factory?

"Right," said Mary, "so what about motive? That might give us a lead to what happened after he was kidnapped."

Amanda chipped in. "Mr Patten told me once that a long time ago he had been dead keen on finding clues, and had been quite good at it. He came into Reception and found me on my knees under the table looking for an earring and asked me a few questions – trying to help, you see. Anyway, I remember, he told me that the most unlikely place to have lost something is where I discovered I'd lost it. And he was quite right. I found the earring back home on my bedroom floor."

We digested this new insight into Francis Patten as we sipped our drinks in the Chequers. That certainly seemed to fit with his intricate knowledge and interest in collecting small valuable objects, which would have involved detailed research into tracing their history and provenance.

Suddenly, Edward slammed down his tankard onto the slightly sticky pub tabletop.

"Amanda!" he exclaimed. "Brilliant girl. You've jolted my memory about something Francis said to me, donkey's years ago." He gathered his thoughts.

"He's about sixty years old, I guess, so would have been early twenties in the last war. We had been briefly reminiscing here in this room about our respective war experiences. I'm about his age and had been out in Egypt and North Africa with the infantry much of the time.

"Francis seemed reluctant to tell me much, but that is his character. However, he did say that his war was home here in Blighty, working for the London Signals Intelligence Centre.

"Now, it's not common knowledge, but I happen to know from one of my old Army colleagues that this so-called signals centre was using a dilapidated old mansion house well outside London, called Bletchley Park. Apparently, all kinds of clever goings-on happened there during the war – nobody really knows what these days. I wonder. Maybe there's more to our Francis than we ever imagined."

CHAPTER EIGHTEEN

PLANS FOR THE FUTURE ON THE WAY TO LONDON

Of course, I'm writing this story about half a century after the conversation that I have just recorded, and today we know all about Bletchley Park. Even those wartime occupants of its offices and workrooms, who had been sworn to secrecy, have in recent years felt able to abandon the total silence they have hitherto maintained so magnificently, and have begun to reveal their various roles at the time. But in the 1970s, less than thirty years after the war itself, their lips remained sealed.

Edward, Mary and Amanda had latched onto Edward's revelation in the pub and had decided that under the heading 'Likely' on Mary's checklist, it should be recorded that Francis had not merely been a victim of kidnap. They had concluded that he was possibly an agent of the very security forces who were pursuing the right-wing extremists. This would account for his motive in driving to Royston.

It might also provide another explanation for his non-appearance in recent months. Might his official role have been discovered by Hatcher or his superiors, and he had then been murdered?

Or, had he been instructed to get himself caught and held by the Royston gang, and to persuade them to believe that he was an admirer of their political philosophy and wished to join them? The security services would then have a 'mole' on the inside.

I have to admit that I thought this whole idea of Francis as a spook for MI5, ever since WWII, a complete flight of fancy. We were letting our imaginations run riot. All very exciting, but surely the real-life scenario would be much more boring and prosaic.

However, I was in the minority, and Mary's 'Action' column now had only one entry: Find someone who might know.

If their hunch was correct, then obviously it was pointless to try to extract any information from our friend Detective Inspector Mason, who would have been briefed from on high about any such role for Francis. Indeed, any suspicion by the police that a group of Francis's colleagues had uncovered his MI5 connection could have been very awkward for us.

Who else might have their ear to the ground?

Then I remembered my conversation months before, with the Church clerk at the Scientologists in Southend, the chap called Robert. He had mentioned his son Roy, a journalist with the local paper, who had delved deep into the case of the Vietnamese orphans, and had helped the police track down the criminals involved. Might he be able and willing to pursue some undercover enquiries?

There was only one way to find out.

The following Sunday I visited once again the Church of Christ Scientist on the green outskirts of Southend. I was welcomed as before and was relieved to find that Robert was present. After the service, I joined him for coffee.

No, he had heard nothing at all about Francis's disappearance. It was all very worrying.

"Well," I explained, "some of my colleagues and I at Hoffmann's have been doing some hard thinking. We have become convinced," (I generously bowed to the majority view) "that there is more to it than his mere curiosity. We wondered if your son Roy might be able to help us, as he was very much involved in the Vietnamese orphan scandal. Could you tell me how I could get in touch with him?"

"Certainly, my young friend," replied Robert. "Roy is no longer in Southend. He was offered a post as investigative journalist for the *Daily Mail* in London. I'll give you his phone number at home, or you can find him at the *Mail*."

*

WHERE IS FRANCIS?

A few days later, Mr Nicolas called me into his office.

"Sit down, Richard, sit down. No need to stand on ceremony. Now, young man, you have been with us here for long enough for me to gauge your potential with my firm. Apart from your very conservative sartorial tastes, and apparent reluctance to wear our BHS shirts as often as I would like, you have picked up the shop-floor management of this factory rather well.

"As you will have seen in the newspaper, no doubt, my last factory manager has been dispatched to a lengthy period in prison, and will certainly never again be in my employ. I need a new manager and, with a little guidance, you can be that man.

"I have arranged for my experienced manager at Barnstaple, Adrian Bingham, to take you under his wing there for about two months to learn the ropes, and then you can return here, if all goes well, to take charge of the factory. I will then remain here for a few weeks to monitor your progress, and after that will return to London.

"In the meantime, I have arranged with British Home Stores that their other shirt supplier, Gerrards Limited, will temporarily share their style designer with us, at a regrettable fee, until Francis Patten can resume his duties. I very much hope that will be quite soon.

"So, Richard Trahair, are you up for it?"

What could I say? Of course I was happy to be sent to Barnstaple – only an hour and three quarters drive down to my family home across Dartmoor. I knew in my heart, however, that I would never be returning to Essex if it involved making shirts, or indeed any other garment. I had already received from the College of Estate Management in Reading their comprehensive set of excellent textbooks between blue covers pertaining to forestry, agricultural tenancies, land surveying, property law, designing cattle grids, rural estate economy, and animal diseases; and had ordered the latest edition of *Scammell*.

"I say, Mr Nicolas," I replied with as much ingenuous enthusiasm as I could muster, "thank you very much. I shall be delighted to go to Barnstaple and work with Mr Bingham for a couple of months."

I left it at that. No point in upsetting the boss while still in Essex. Besides, I was rather chuffed that such an important man in his field should think that highly of me. I was genuinely grateful.

I was, however, very loath to leave my friends until we had unravelled the mystery of the missing Francis, and I was determined to accelerate our efforts.

I phoned Roy the journalist and arranged to meet him in a pub in Fleet Street one Saturday lunchtime. Edward could not make that date, but Amanda and I took the train into Central London to make a day of it.

On the way, I broke it to her that I was off shortly to the Barnstaple factory for two months.

"But you may be back, Richard?" she replied. "I'll miss you, y'know." She looked at me rather beseechingly. My heart lurched a bit. She was the first girl I had ever been remotely fond of; 'romantically inclined' as my grandmother would have put it.

"Well, Mandy. The thing is…" I hesitated, momentarily lost for words. "The thing is that I don't think I'm really cut out for factory life in the long-term. I'm… well, I'm so fond of you, it's hard to know what to say. And Betty's been a dear. Edward and Mary have kept me sane, too, and I shall – would – miss them all.

"But I need to return to Devon and Cornwall. I'm not really a fan of Essex, least of all Southend and Billericay. I'm going to train as a chartered surveyor in rural estate management and will probably need to live back at home with my parents while I swot for the exams and look for my first trainee job.

"I will work at the Barnstaple factory as I have promised, and do my best, but will probably give Mr Nicolas my notice after a month or so."

I stopped talking and gazed quite unseeingly out of the window at the endless rows of small terraced houses and shabby back gardens that lined the dirty railway line for mile after mile.

Without turning back, I felt Amanda's head on my shoulder, and she took my hand in hers. "Well," she whispered in a small soft voice, "I understand, and I knew this couldn't have lasted. We both have separate ways to go. I wouldn't have missed it for anything, you know. But soon you'll be living back in the leafy countryside, hobnobbing with all the gentry of Devon. Will you remember me then, Richard, dear?"

I squeezed her hand. "I won't ever forget you, Mandy, not ever. It's been such fun."

PLANS FOR THE FUTURE ON THE WAY TO LONDON

I changed tack as we slowed down on the approach to Blackfriars station. "In the meantime, you and I have a job to do here in London," I said, trying to be a bit more cheerful. "Let's go and summon the national press in our search for Francis. I can't leave till I know what's happened, that's for sure."

As arranged, we found The Harrow in Whitefriars off Fleet Street and looked around the sea of newspaper men – or the pond of eccentrics, as I referred to them later – gathering their daily dose of gossip and scandal from one another. We were searching for a red beard, the identifying feature that Roy had given me over the telephone. There seemed to be only one on display, and so we headed for his otherwise empty corner table.

Introductions made, Roy bought us some drinks and we settled down to our task.

We explained our latest discoveries and hunches, bringing Roy fully up to date. He listened with keen interest.

After considering the question over another small whisky and lemon, he mused aloud. "Of course, identifying a field agent in the SIS, or MI5, would be very difficult for a member of the more reputable press," (in which he appeared to include the *Daily Mail*) "and so my best plan will be to approach this investigation with a proper search for Mr Patten himself, using my official and undercover contacts.

"On the question of whether he is dead or alive, my present view is that he is much more likely still to be extant, and has gone to ground on the orders of his superiors. So, my young friends, leave this with me for a week or two, and I will let you know what I discover. There could be something newsworthy in this, so it is all part of a day's work.

"Now, if you will excuse me, I must dash, as I have an editorial meeting back at Northcliffe House."

With that, Roy was gone, and we were left nursing our beer and shandy under the dim light of our corner table. The noise level in The Harrow was terrific, the newsmen downing alcohol in eye-watering quantities with no apparent effect on their ability to shout or mutter their snippets of news and conspiracies at length.

Amanda enjoyed watching this, but I was beginning to get bored. I gazed around at this bevy of Fleet Street regulars in their city suits and ties with some distaste.

After a while, I became conscious of one individual in particular, standing on his own with a small glass in hand at the far end of the bar, speaking to no one. What grasped my attention was that whenever I looked his way, he quickly averted his eyes away from us and pretended to concentrate his gaze on features of the pub around him, in a singularly unconvincing manner.

I realised that he had come into the pub shortly after us and, thinking about it, I also had a feeling that I had seen him on the railway platform when we had got off the train.

I nudged Amanda alongside me at the pub table.

"I rather think we have been followed," I said to her

PLANS FOR THE FUTURE ON THE WAY TO LONDON

quietly. "Don't look now, but there's a man down the far end who is taking more interest in us than I like."

She turned to me with wide eyes and an impish grin.

"Gosh, Richard, what have you got me into now, you wicked boy?"

CHAPTER NINETEEN
WARNINGS OF DANGER

I don't know what prompted me to be so rash. Maybe I was trying to impress my girlfriend as a swashbuckling strongman or something equally inappropriate, but I couldn't resist it.

We rose quickly from our table in the pub and strolled towards the entrance. This meant passing, within a foot or two, the mysterious stranger who had been staring at us over his whisky glass. As I walked past him I murmured, "Give my regards to MI5, my dear sir."

I rather spoilt the effect by turning round after a few seconds and giving the man a rather sheepish smirk. He was looking at me in blank amazement and then plonked his glass onto the bar top and caught us up as we set off down the street.

"Just one moment, you two."

We stopped.

He then extracted from his pocket a black wallet which I instantly recognised from my earlier experiences as an Essex Constabulary warrant card.

"Harvey, Essex CID. A quick word with you, young sleuths. Well done for noticing me, but this isn't a game, you know. Inspector Mason has instructed me to keep an eye on you from time to time to save you from any mischief. And no, I am not a member of MI5, just an ordinary police officer acting in your own interests.

"I know what you're up to. You want the *Daily Mail* to help find your missing colleague. I happen to know that journalist; I had dealings with him when he worked in Southend. Well, I can tell you now that he too will shortly be receiving a visit from a police officer, and if he has any sense he will agree to back off."

I interrupted. "But why?" I blurted out. "Why can't he help us? I sometimes wonder if the police are really trying to find Francis at all. You don't tell us anything about how any official search is going. That's why we and other colleagues of his feel we have to keep on looking. We're beginning to think there's something odd going on."

Detective Constable Harvey was a sympathetic sort and had not long been in the police service. He had not yet developed the deadpan, non-committal response to awkward questions from members of the public that his more experienced colleagues adopted, to steer their way through the maze of public service and official secrecy that had to be negotiated each working day.

For a moment, he looked nonplussed, clearly struggling to find the right reply to my outburst.

Amanda and I stared at him expectantly.

Silence.

"Listen, you two," he eventually said. He paused again. "Right, now then. All I can tell you is that the relevant authorities know full well what Mr Patten has been doing since his absence from work at your factory. Sorry, but I can't tell you anything more than that. Now go home, and rest assured that the matter is being fully dealt with. No more James Bond stuff, OK?"

*

"But hang on," interposed Edward when, once more, I was sitting in his drawing room with a glass of sherry. "DC Harvey didn't actually say whether Francis was somewhere safe, or somewhere at risk, did he?"

I had gone round to Mary and Edward as soon as Amanda and I had returned from London and had reported all that had occurred.

"Nope," I acknowledged, "we're still in the dark."

Just then, the phone rang and Mary went out into the hall to answer it.

The drawing room door was open and Edward and I heard the one-sided conversation.

"Hello, Hanningfield 3471?" said Mary, the receiver to her ear. "Yes, speaking… Detective Inspector Mason, did you say? Yes, he is here with me and the colonel,

Inspector. Really? Good gracious me. Well alright, and we will expect you here shortly. Goodbye."

She returned to the room.

Edward looked up as she entered.

"What on earth was all that about?"

Mary had gone quite pale. "That was the police wanting to know if Richard was with us. They are coming straight here, and in the meantime we should lock the doors and permit no one else into the house. Apparently Richard is in danger."

We all three looked at each other in blank amazement. In danger? The idea was surely absurd.

Edward suddenly jumped up and went into his study, emerging swiftly with his old service revolver which he tucked into his jacket pocket.

"No ammo, but it might scare off any intruder," he explained with a grim smile.

Mary cast her eyes heavenwards. "Oh really, Edward, do be sensible."

None of us could think of anything more to say, so we sat in silence until, five minutes later, the doorbell clanged. Edward rose to answer it, his hand in his jacket pocket.

He returned with DI Mason and another man, middle-aged and in a grey suit, with a rather forgettable facial appearance.

Mason opened the conversation. "Well, young man," he said, addressing me, "for a change, I am not here to tick you off for meddling in police affairs or trying to be a private detective, along with your girlfriend and the colonel and his wife here.

"I want you to cast your mind back to 1968 when you were still living at home near Tavistock in Devon. You will remember that you stood in for your father on one occasion and delivered a spare part to a foreign ship that had arrived in Plymouth."

"Of course I remember," I butted in, "the Iron Shackle Fraternity."

The man in the grey suit looked up at me sharply but said nothing.

Mason continued. "You remember the young Polish chap who showed you around his ship?"

"I do, rather a distinctive fellow. I would easily recognise him again I expect, although it was several years ago, of course. It's a funny coincidence you asking me all this, because I was only reminiscing over the same event with my boss's brother the other day. Mr Daniel."

Again, the grey suit pierced me with his surprisingly penetrating glance.

Mason cleared his throat and paused, with a brief look towards his colleague.

"Ah, well, coincidence indeed," he continued hastily, "but I have to inform you that this Polish sailor has been on the run in this country ever since, and the authorities have reason to believe that he has been engaged in activity contrary to our national interests, and is now evading arrest by our intelligence services." Here again, Mason exchanged a glance with Grey Suit.

"He is likely to go to any lengths, including violence, I regret to say, to avoid being recognised. Now, he is understood at present to be in this part of the country and may well be trying to find you, Richard, as you are one of the very few people who would know him and who might remember the conversations you had with him on the ship."

"You mean his curious interest in getting to somewhere near Malvern?" I asked.

Grey Suit shot me yet another of his flashing glances.

"Yes, quite," responded the inspector. "Quite so, and maybe other clues to his intentions that you might yet remember. If he found you, he might take steps to, um, prevent you from recalling anything that could prove useful to the, er, authorities in achieving a successful prosecution."

Mary interrupted. "A spy then, Inspector?"

"More than that, I'm afraid, madam; this man is also a key player in a recent high-level attempt to disrupt our democratic state order, and—"

Grey Suit interrupted the police officer, speaking for the first time since they had arrived.

"Nothing further on that, please, Inspector. Suffice it to say that this Polish man is dangerous in more than one respect. Now, we'll leave it at that."

Mason nodded in acknowledgment.

"Richard, we are putting you under police protection until this offender has been apprehended. Don't worry, go about your work and recreation as usual, but don't be surprised to see Detective Constable Harvey – whom I believe you have already met – shadowing you at all times. At night, there will be separate police monitor operations covering your home in Billericay. Now, if you will excuse us, we will leave you in peace to enjoy the rest of your evening."

With that, the two figures of authority departed.

"Bloody hell," pronounced Edward, after we had sat in stunned silence for several minutes.

Mary frowned at him and said she would go and make coffee.

"You and I need more than coffee, Richard," Edward stated rather firmly, "a stiff whisky is more the thing, I think," and he went in search of the decanter.

CHAPTER TWENTY

FAREWELLS, WITH A NASTY SURPRISE

It was about a week later that Mr Nicolas called me into his office at the factory.

"Richard, I have arranged with Adrian Bingham in Barnstaple to take you on at my factory there from next Monday. You will have to arrange accommodation there promptly, but Bingham suggests that you telephone him today, and he can book you in temporarily at a small private hotel in the town until you find somewhere settled for your two month training down there.

"That's all, and I wish you well. You have the makings of a good general manager, and who knows? You could do well in this trade if you put your mind to it."

I left his office in some anxiety. Not only would I have to break the news to my bungalow landlord, who would have little time to find a new poodle-sitter, but also I had to speak to DC Harvey or DI Mason about my 'police protection' being transferred to the Devonshire Constabulary.

Not to mention saying goodbye to my new dear friends Edward, Mary and Betty.

And my heart sank at the prospect of parting from Amanda.

I knew that I would never be returning to Essex. This extraordinary chapter of my life was going to end abruptly in a week's time, my close relationships suddenly severed and a new life, before very long, commencing back in Devon in an entirely new career and environment.

I left Mr Nicolas's office with all these thoughts ricocheting off each other in a rather confused jumble.

I looked back briefly at the closed door of his office.

I would never see Nicolas Hoffmann again. Along with his brother Daniel, he was now part of my history. At the age of twenty-two, this seemed to me a sad concept after all that they had invested in me for a career that I was now to abandon.

I often wonder today what happened to the Hoffmann enterprise, and all its staff, grumbling or loyal, now that BHS itself is a relic of the past.

*

On the Thursday before I was to depart, Edward and Mary very kindly laid on a farewell dinner for me at their cottage. I arrived to find, to my surprise and delight, a

FAREWELLS, WITH A NASTY SURPRISE

huge welcome party comprising not only my hosts but Betty and her husband Ernie; dear old Albert, the now retired lay designer; and, of course, Amanda, who was placed very promptly next to me at the genuine Georgian dining table glistening with Waterford Crystal and polished silver in the centre of the spacious dining room.

Edward made a speech, mercifully short, and proposed a toast to our absent colleague Francis who, in more favourable circumstances, would also have been present.

Betty and Ernie had brought Amanda along in their old Austin A40, but I whispered to her as we drank our coffee, "I'll take you home, Mandy, and we'll go back to my place first for a glass or two of something so we can say goodbye properly. I've got to drive back home to Devon tomorrow and might not see you before…" I faltered with a huge lump in my throat. "Well, before I leave Billericay at lunchtime, and there may not be a chance to… well… say anything." I gave up the unequal struggle, and Amanda slid her hand beneath the mahogany tabletop and squeezed my wrist. We exchanged sad smiles but I spotted a single teardrop from the corner of her left eye run slowly down her smooth cheek before she quickly wiped it away and looked around at her fellow guests in embarrassment. No one noticed.

After all the thank yous, handshakes and hugs in the hall, as we donned our coats and hats to meet the pouring rain outside, Amanda and I got into the Saab and, with a cheery wave to Edward and Mary out of the car window, I drove off back to Billericay.

WHERE IS FRANCIS?

It was rather late by the time we got back to my bungalow, mine for only one more night.

I presumed that Constable Harvey had long gone off duty, and that the night shift of police protection – whatever that was – would now be in operation.

Amanda and I walked up the concrete pathway to the front door in pitch blackness. As we approached, I could hear my protégé standard poodle indoors, growling and muttering to himself.

"Listen to poor pooch; I've never heard him do that before. Maybe he's crossing his legs and fit to burst. We'd better let him out a bit quick."

I found my Yale key and shoved it into the lock.

The door swung open before I had a chance to turn the key. The latch groaned and fell onto the doorstep with a clatter.

The dog ran out and licked my hand. Amanda grabbed my arm. "Richard, someone's bust the door. You've had a break-in."

I stepped cautiously over the threshold and reached around the door frame for the light switch.

The narrow hallway lit up and we both padded silently over the lino floor to the door at the far end, which was the only one ajar. This was the sitting room where I had fully intended to share our farewells together in a manner inevitably restrained by my 1970s sheltered concept of appropriate romance: a cuddle and a few kisses. Perhaps I had hoped that Amanda's idea of what was appropriate would be along the same lines.

FAREWELLS, WITH A NASTY SURPRISE

But either way, it was not to be.

Again, I paused in the doorway and slid my hand around to the light switch, as the room was in darkness.

The central ceiling light under its turquoise plastic lampshade snapped on. Seated in my vinyl armchair opposite, facing the door, sat a tall, gaunt man with long, dirty, yellow hair and an unhealthily pale face, his right hand extended towards me at chest level, gripping an automatic pistol. The black hole of its barrel I could discern all too clearly.

Amanda let out a yelp and gripped my arm again but then stood defiantly alongside me.

Of course, instantly I knew who he was: my old Polish guide around the clipper ship in Millbay Docks in 1968. He had evidently lived a fairly rough life since that first acquaintance. Equally instantly, I knew that I must at all costs, indicate that he was a complete stranger to me.

He said nothing, and I said nothing. I toyed with a Wodehousian reaction of raised eyebrow and, 'to what do we owe the privilege of this courteous greeting?' but thought better of it.

I could see that the Pole was disconcerted by the presence of a girl. This was evidently not a scenario that he had expected.

After a few moments, he barked, "Siddown," and waved us, with his gun, towards the sofa at the side of the room.

"I have nothing here of any value," I protested, "and no money or anything. This isn't my house – I'm just renting it furnished." Quite why I elaborated on to estate agent's particulars, I don't know. I guess I was just gabbling something while my brain feverishly worked overtime to find a way out of this decidedly tricky situation.

"Could you please leave my home immediately. Your attempted burglary has failed, and you have broken the front door latch and lock which I will now have to get replaced tomorrow morning."

I realised his game at this point, as he continued to say nothing. He was putting me to the test by using his silence to prompt me to talk and give the game away. Nonetheless, from what Inspector Mason had said, ultimately, the Pole needed to eliminate me as a potential prosecution witness for my conversation with the man in 1968. Nothing I said to him now would alter that fact.

Where the heck were my police protectors? There must have been an administrative hiccup and they had failed to turn up. I couldn't help glancing across at the telephone on its little table in the corner. Mr Yellow Hair watched me and smirked evilly.

"Please, sir," piped up Amanda, "take what you want and just leave. Please?" She had no idea of the unspoken communications beaming to and fro across the sitting room. I had never thought to tell her about my adventure with the Iron Shackle Fraternity all those years ago. She must have assumed that this intruder was an armed burglar, and nothing more, which was bad enough.

Well, something had to break this hiatus. We had been sitting there on tenterhooks for at least ten minutes,

FAREWELLS, WITH A NASTY SURPRISE

and all the Pole had said so far was 'Siddown'. I had to play for time.

The front door was still hanging open, and in the light from the hallway I hoped that the broken lock would be clearly visible from the road or pathway. Surely the police would come soon.

Then Yellow Hair seemed to make up his mind about something. He shifted in his seat and lowered his pistol. "You do not remember me, I think." His accent was East European staccato. "We had a little conversation a long way ago on a sail ship in Plymouth Sound. You had brung a engine part to me, I shown you round the ship. Ya?"

I pretended to look puzzled. Amanda had no need to pretend. She looked mystified.

Just at that point, my pulse began to race. There was a small window next to the fireplace, behind the Pole's chair. The curtains in the room had not been drawn, and in that moment I could have sworn I spotted a movement, some darker shadow flitting across the blackness of the glass outside.

I answered him, having to clear my throat and draw breath several times first. "I remember the clipper ship, yes. I had a wonderful welcome from the crew on board. Were you one of them? What did we talk about? I don't recall."

"I am a reasonable man," he replied. "I will tell you why it is necessary to do what I am about to do. I am sorry, but my own life may depend on it."

I turned to Amanda and took her hand in mine, trying to smile encouragingly but probably without success.

The Pole then proceeded, in his halting English, to reveal in proud detail his escape from the clipper ship and his nefarious commission from the Soviet authorities to infiltrate the British security services by teaming up with existing assorted spies, traitors and revolutionaries of totalitarian motive to disrupt the civil state and weaken its intelligence capability in whatever way they could find.

"And now, I is on the run. Your secret services and policja are tracking me down and may catch me to arrest me, and zoof, I might be in jail the rest of my life. So I must be shot – as you say? – of all witnesses. I have, ha ha, shot several already."

Again, the spine-chilling smirk.

"But, what to do with this fine young lady? I am thinking about it."

There was definitely someone outside that little window by the fireplace. Then I saw a torch beam briefly flashed twice. The sitting room door into the hallway was closed, but I could see out of the corner of my eye that it was very slightly ajar. Maybe Amanda could make a sudden dash for it if I managed to distract Yellow Hair for a few seconds.

Suddenly, this proved unnecessary. A piercing, high-decibel whistle, extremely painful on the ears, hit the air in the room that instant, prompting all three of us instinctively to clamp our hands to the side of our head. The sound was physically intolerable.

Simultaneously, the glass in the small window shattered and something fast and solid hit the Pole on the back of the head, which made him slump forward, dropping his pistol.

Quick-witted Amanda leapt up and kicked the gun across the carpet to the far side of the room, just as the sitting room door flew open and three men in commando khaki and army berets burst in and literally threw Amanda and me to the floor, then surrounded the Pole with three Webley service revolvers pointing inches from his face.

Within seconds, he too was on the floor, but in his case with face buried in the nylon hearthrug and his arms strapped behind him with wrists in tight handcuffs.

Mercifully, the debilitating, high-pitched whistle then stopped. All was momentarily silent except for the tinkling of a few large slivers of window glass still toppling sporadically out of their putty onto the window sill.

For some reason, my bungalow landlord came to mind. When he came home on Saturday to collect his poodle, he will think his tenant had suddenly gone berserk and started to destroy his property. I giggled inanely and helped Amanda to her feet, back onto the sofa.

The soldiers hauled the Pole to his feet and led him out of the room and along the hall corridor, without a word being spoken.

Amanda and I were left there on our own, sitting in what was now a howling draught from the smashed window and the wide-open front door. We had wrapped our arms around one another and were both shaking, not just from the cold air.

"As I was about to suggest before we were so rudely interrupted," I began, "how about a small glass of brandy and lemon, you poor girl. I'll switch the fireplace on."

I flicked on both electric bars, the extravagance eminently justified.

Then the front door banged shut, and we heard footsteps approaching down the passage. Inspector Mason came into the room, smiling broadly.

"Sorry to put you both through that," he said. "It was a risk, but I hope you will accept that it was worthwhile when we have explained what, with your help, we have now achieved. I'll leave that to my colleague here, whom I think you may recognise."

And into the room walked Francis Patten.

CHAPTER TWENTY-ONE
REVELATION AND RALLENTANDO

You may well imagine the sheer surprise with which Amanda and I rose to meet our long-lost colleague, as though some kind of apparition had materialised out of the blue, or, in this case, at about half past eleven, out of the black of a cold, wet night.

Francis strode forward to greet us hand outstretched. "My dear young friends, I cannot tell you what great pleasure this brings me, and such relief as well. In the last few weeks, Detective Inspector Mason has been keeping me up to date with your brave attempts to find me, and fearing the worst, over so many months. Edward and Mary Hanson too. I shall be seeing them both tomorrow. I am so sorry that, for reasons I will try to explain, I have been unable to contact you all recently to put your minds at rest. Let's sit down, and I can tell you all."

I went across to the melamine-and-chipboard drinks cabinet and extracted three glasses and a selection of bottles. The inspector had quietly withdrawn and had gone on his way.

Amanda drew all the curtains to induce a more cosy atmosphere, and we pulled our chairs and sofa nearer to the pathetic electric fire.

"Incidentally," Francis began, "I made my peace with Mr Nicolas yesterday morning, on the telephone. He readily agreed to say nothing to anybody until I give the word tomorrow.

"Oh, thanks, Richard. I'll have a glass of that soda water please. I'm teetotal, you understand.

"Now, the first thing to show you is this rather clever little machine."

He extracted from his jacket pocket a metal box with a small aperture and hinged lid that looked most sophisticated.

"This is a battery-operated Sony TC50 recorder which has had its innards tweaked to strengthen the microphone pickup range and power. I have been holding it up against the glass of that little window there all the time that you and the intruder were talking. It has, I'm pleased to say, caught every word of that man's boastful admissions to you, with complete clarity. Thanks to your skill, both of you, in leading him to tell you all that – as we had hoped he would – the prosecution evidence against him looks watertight and may well help the authorities find some of the other conspirators he has worked with. A grand job, both of you."

And he raised his glass in a silent toast.

Francis sat back for a moment to collect his thoughts, and then for the next forty-five minutes explained what he had been up to since I last spoke to him about that dodgy parcel delivery in his factory office all those months ago.

*

He had been intrigued about that delivery. It had sounded all wrong. At first, his concern had been for the Hoffmann company's interests, but there quickly developed another motive.

"I can't say too much about this, I'm afraid, and it's necessary to explain that I am subject to the Official Secrets Act. Ever since my role during the war, I have been assisting the authorities in their undercover work for state security. You were all spot on with that guess, which you told Mason about.

"I can tell you that now, because this has been my final task in that connection and I am now officially discharged. Well, I will be on Monday. I have always insisted I would stop when I reached sixty."

Francis had checked in with his security contact, on the way up to Royston in his Alvis, and had been told to go ahead and investigate, if necessary, from the inside. He had knocked on the door of the mansion and had raised a similar query over the parcel delivery as I had.

"Unfortunately, I'm not as quick on my feet as you,

Richard, and I was hustled indoors by this surprisingly strong woman. I was hauled down into the basement and locked in a cellar just beyond the exhibition room with all that Fascist memorabilia. I had plenty of time to put two and two together while incarcerated there and realised that the selling of Vietnamese orphans was a side issue to the state conspiracy.

"Then, after a long time in that miserable hole, I was suddenly carted off in handcuffs and blindfold one night in a Transit van, and driven some distance to another house, which I later discovered was in Harlow.

"Well, to cut a long story short, I managed to escape early one morning through a sash window that had a faulty latch and, unlike all the others, had not been nailed shut.

"I made my way to London and reported for duty with my security contact, and was commissioned to pursue the case. You'd be surprised if you knew who my security contact was, but I'm not going to tell you!

"Anyway, from that point on, I had, of course, to remain completely incommunicado with all my colleagues and friends at church and at the factory and elsewhere, which was very frustrating but unavoidable.

"The police themselves were not informed of my role or whereabouts until only a few weeks ago, and so spent the first few months genuinely searching for me. But I had long been taught how to make myself invisible.

"About three weeks ago, I was tasked with finding and cornering the Polish absconder from your Plymouth clipper ship – what an extraordinary coincidence that was, Richard – which proved remarkably easy. He's not very bright, that chap.

"Well, my superiors then had the idea of steering the Pole down here to Billericay with a few oblique clues that you were here, and then to set a trap. I have to say I was dead against that idea; far too risky for your own safety. The Essex Police were also rather unhappy until Mason was given permission to set up police protection with your knowledge.

"Of course, we were shadowing the Pole all the time, but knew he was armed. I didn't like it one bit. I think that Amanda turning up with you this evening reduced the risk considerably.

"Well," Francis concluded, slapping his hands on his knees and standing up, "that's about it, and I must leave you in peace, and go and get a few hours' sleep before picking up the pieces with my normal life once again.

"I gather you are off west for a while, my good friend, and so I will wish you farewell." We shook hands.

And he was gone.

*

Amanda and I sat there on the sofa, musing over these momentous events, and sipping from our miniature glasses of spirits (the glasses emblazoned on their sides with 'A gift from sunny Southend-on-Sea' around the rim).

Then the door creaked open and the dog padded into the room with the distinctly puzzled face of a poodle wishing to be informed of the reason for his highly disturbed night that had deprived him of any sleep and hoping that a few doggy treats might go a long way to rectifying matters.

I looked at my watch. Twenty past midnight.

I realised that Amanda and I were still in the same tight embrace that we had resumed when Francis had begun his story.

"I'd better go home." She sighed. "I'm on at Reception again at nine o'clock. Will you run me back, Richard? We both need a bit of a kip."

I drained my glass and took a deep breath, resting my head on her soft shoulder.

"I guess so, my sweet Mandy," I replied a little dismally.

And so, once again and for the last time, we travelled in the green Saab together, trying to hold hands between gear changes.

"My, that was a lengthy farewell dinner, you two," exclaimed Amanda's elder sister with whom she shared a tiny flat the other side of town. "I was getting worried."

Amanda and I exchanged sheepish grins and said nothing. She went indoors with her sister, and I returned to the car, sitting there in the driver's seat in pitch darkness for quite a long time.

A light went on in one of the windows of the flat, and the silhouette of a familiar, dear figure was framed there for some moments. She raised a hand briefly in a little wave. She knew I was there. Then the curtains were drawn across the stage, the final scene of the final act bringing to a close the most extraordinary drama I could ever have experienced or imagined. To this day, I remain uncertain which had been fact and which had been fiction. It was all so long ago, so very long ago.

I can never now be certain what, in truth, was hidden in the curiously heavy parcel I delivered that day into the hands of a small child in a doorway in the town of Royston.

ACKNOWLEDGEMENTS

I am, as ever, indebted to all the team at The Book Guild for their unfailing encouragement, courtesy and thoroughness in the production of this book.

ABOUT THE AUTHOR

Richard Trahair studied Textile Management at the University of Leeds in the 1970s before qualifying in rural estate management as a chartered surveyor and agricultural land agent. Retiring in 2011, he has written four novels and a light-hearted memoir about property management in the Church of England.